*"So you're t...
Kyle Tremor...*

Kyle nodded. "You shed your blonde locks pretty quick. Are you a natural redhead?"

"No."

She didn't elaborate, which stirred his imagination. When he realised how curious he was to know more about this woman, he abruptly halted the direction of his thoughts. "Do you have a name?" he asked, studying her profile.

She hesitated. Kyle found himself wanting her to trust him and annoyed that it mattered. He grew increasingly aware of her scent, the warmth radiating from her body, the soft, even sound of her breathing. His senses absorbed everything about her in an intense, disturbing fashion, even while he argued the idiocy of the reaction.

"You can call me Rianna, if you'd like."

He liked.

Available in March 2005 from Silhouette Sensation

Undercover Virgin

BECKY BARKER

SILHOUETTE®
Sensation™

*Silhouette, Silhouette Sensation and Colophon are
registered trademarks of Harlequin Books S.A., used under licence.*

*First published in Great Britain 2005
Silhouette Books, Eton House, 18-24 Paradise Road,
Richmond, Surrey TW9 1SR*

© Rebecca L Barker 2004

ISBN 0 373 27348 7

18-0305

*Printed and bound in Spain
by Litografía Rosés S.A., Barcelona*

BECKY BARKER

is a multipublished author whose novels have been translated into more than a dozen languages.

Her personal hero is a former marine who helped her create three terrific children. Rachel and her husband, Jerramy; Amanda and her husband, Jay; and Thad and his wife, Dara, all live within a few miles of Mum and Dad in rural Ohio.

Besides spending time with her family, Becky enjoys music, gardening and reading. She loves to hear from readers and can be reached at PO Box 113, Mt Sterling, OH, 43143, USA or through her website at www.BeckyBarker.com.

I'd like to dedicate this book to my siblings
and their spouses, because the older I get, the more I
value them and our big, extended family. With love to
Judy and Randy, Cathy and Larry, Tim and Luana,
Thom and Sue, Peggy and in memory of Michael.
Also, with love to Dee Dee, Sue and Dave.

And as always, special thanks to Buzz,
the wind beneath my wings!

Chapter 1

It had been too easy. Too damn easy, thought Kyle Tremont as he surveyed the elegant ballroom of Gregory Haroldson's estate. The plan to get him into the employ of the wealthy banker had come together without a hitch. It had all gone like a perfectly choreographed dance.

The ease of it only made him edgy and more vigilant.

Some unseen sharpshooter had taken a wild shot at Haroldson, and Kyle had been on hand to shield the other man with his body. Instant gratitude and a generous job offer. Kyle had wondered, several times, why he hadn't shoved Haroldson into the path of the bullet. Dead was a more sure-fire way to punish a man than the prospect of a jail term.

Only five days into the operation, and he wanted out. He'd cursed himself a thousand times over for letting Donald Sullivan coerce him into helping. The daily doses of Haroldson's arrogance were more than he could stomach. The urge to strangle the man with his bare hands grew stronger every time he laid eyes on him.

Undercover work had definitely lost its appeal. The innate hunger for a challenge that had motivated him in his younger days was nonexistent now. He had retired four years ago when the taste for intrigue died along with his partner.

Despite being on Haroldson's payroll, he'd yet to be contacted by the elusive agent with the code name Phantom. His assignment was to help the undercover FBI agent escape Haroldson's heavily guarded compound. Deputy Director Sullivan had lured him out of retirement with a promise that Phantom had gathered enough concrete evidence to make Haroldson pay for his crimes.

Kyle was tired of waiting and at risk of losing his patience altogether.

"She's a first-class babe, ain't she."

Kyle glanced at his fellow employee. Damon was young, cocky and a little dim-witted, but basically an okay guy. The two of them were usually paired as driver and bodyguard for high-ranking members of Haroldson's little empire.

Tonight, they were enjoying the annual staff appreciation dinner. Haroldson knew how to keep his people happy and loyal by pretending they were important to him. The ballroom's many chandeliers had been dimmed to a soft, intimate glow. Food was abundant, booze flowed freely and a small orchestra played music for dancing.

Damon's admiring gaze was fastened on their hostess for the evening.

"You mean Haroldson's fiancée?"

"She's a real knockout, and damn nice, too. Always doin' something for the staff and their families."

Nice wasn't exactly the word Kyle would use to describe Haroldson's very young, very blond girlfriend. Definitely a May-December relationship. Gossip had it that she'd moved in with him as soon as they'd announced their engagement. Apparently, he adored her and refused her nothing.

"I guess she can afford to be generous."

"Yeah, but I seen plenty of those rich bitches who turn their noses up at guys like us. 'Fraid they'll get dirty if we touch 'em or somethin'. Samantha, she's not that way."

Kyle had never been introduced to the lady in question. Nor did he want to be. He couldn't summon much interest in a woman who'd sleep with a bastard like Haroldson.

"I don't figure I'll be getting up close and personal with the boss's woman."

The younger man laughed. "That's what you think. She's makin' her way toward us now. She and the boss, they have this little routine. When he hires a new employee, she's the one what gets up close and personal. The boss gets a kick out of watchin' the hired help drool. She'll have you pantin' after her in a few minutes."

Oh, hell, thought Kyle. Damon usually knew what he was talking about when it came to his boss's habits. He ground his teeth in frustration. The last thing he needed was attention drawn to him, especially for Haroldson's amusement.

Their hostess slowly made her way through the throng of partygoers, stopping to speak to several peo-

ple as she crossed the room. Everyone wanted a word
with the lady of the manor. He watched her graceful,
unhurried progress and steeled himself to suffer her
attention. It wouldn't do to make his distaste evident.
Better to play the dumb but awed hired hand.

"Damn, but she looks hot in that red dress," muttered Damon. "Too bad she never strays for real. I'd
be first in line to jump her delicate bones."

Haroldson's fiancée wasn't what he'd call petite—
probably five foot seven or eight, with a slender but
generously curved figure. As she drew closer, Kyle's
gaze drifted down her elegant neck, across the bare,
unblemished skin of her shoulders and chest to an en-
ticing view of softly rounded breasts displayed by the
strapless dress.

The full-length evening gown managed to look both
tasteful and wickedly provocative. A man would have
to be dead not to react. Her heavy mane of platinum-
blond hair parted in the middle and framed an oval-
shaped face in feathery layers. Although not classically
beautiful, her features were striking, attractive and en-
hanced to perfection.

The best money could buy. She had to be an un-
principled gold digger who'd sold her soul to the high-
est bidder. That alone should leave him cold, but his
body wasn't listening to common sense. It was just
reacting.

Wide-set, exotically highlighted blue eyes captured
his attention and held his gaze as she came to a stop
in front of him. He felt the impact of her gaze clear to
his toes. Her expensive perfume teased his senses, and
set his nerves alive with reaction. The sizzle of attraction hummed through his veins at the sultry challenge
in those beautiful eyes.

"T. R. O. U. B. L. E." The lyrics to a country-western song popped into his mind. Haroldson's ladylove packed a sensual wallop that could mean nothing but trouble.

"Mr. Jackson." She greeted him by his alias and offered her hand. "I don't believe we've been introduced." Her voice was low and sexy, barely audible above the noise of the party. "I wanted to personally thank you for saving Gregory's life."

Kyle briefly grasped her hand, but kept his grip limp. She responded with a warm, firm grasp. Her touch made his skin sizzle with awareness.

She smiled, transforming her features to unexpected loveliness. It gave him another jolt. Not just because of the physical difference, but because of the genuine warmth and charm she emanated. No wonder she had the staff ready to jump her bones or jump through hoops for her. Warning himself to beware of wolves in sheeps' clothing, he briefly returned the smile.

"It's a pleasure to meet you, ma'am."

"There's no need to call me ma'am. We're all one big family here. My name is Samantha," she said, and then asked, "And your first name is Anthony?"

"Tony's fine."

For this assignment, he was keeping his hair dyed inky black. Thanks to tinted contacts, his blue eyes were temporarily brown. He'd even added a mustache. His naturally dark complexion had always made it easy for him to take on a Mediterranean look.

"Well, Tony, I certainly hope you're enjoying yourself. Did you get enough to eat?"

"Yes, ma'am— I mean Samantha."

She smiled again—a smile meant to reach right into a man and make him relax. Maybe even threaten his control. Kyle felt another unexpected zing of physical awareness, but hardened himself to the response.

"Do you dance, Tony?" she asked.

He glanced toward Damon, who was giving him a cheesy grin and a sly thumbs-up behind her back. Then he looked toward the dance floor. Several couples were shuffling around to a slow tune, but he wasn't eager to join them.

"I'm not much for dancing," he insisted.

Samantha curled her fingers around his forearm, smiled and batted her lashes with the finesse of a siren.

"Please, don't be shy. I promise I won't step on your feet," she teased. "I'd feel honored if you'd share at least one dance with me."

He glanced toward Haroldson. "Sure the boss won't mind?"

Her husky laughter shivered along his nerves. "I promise the boss won't mind. He thinks it's important for a hostess to mingle with her guests."

She gently but firmly led him to a shadowed corner of the dance floor, and then fitted herself snugly against his body. Heat radiated through him at every point of contact. Her hands slid up his chest to settle lightly on his shoulders, and she tilted her head back to study his face.

Kyle returned her steady gaze while his senses feasted on her warmth, the sweetness of her scent and the full, firm breasts pressed against his chest. He slid his hands to her waist and enjoyed the feel of the taut feminine body wrapped in soft, silky fabric. His fingers tightened convulsively.

It felt good to hold her. Really good, yet disturbing. Wrong place, wrong time, wrong woman, his brain insisted while his body vibrated with pleasure. It had been too long since he'd felt such a rush of sexual response to a woman. His deprived hormones were going haywire, but there was no sense fighting the reaction. Might as well enjoy the moment, he thought with a mental shrug.

"Tell me about yourself, Tony," she coaxed, sounding as though she really cared.

He wondered if the attentive attitude was all part of a well-orchestrated game she played with Haroldson. Her lover never made a move without a carefully thought-out plan. Did she support him in his sick games? Would she tempt him with her smile and body, then chuckle about his response in bed tonight?

At the thought, a shaft of anger pierced Kyle, but he swiftly controlled it. Samantha's eyes widened a little, making him wonder if she sensed his tension. Maybe she'd attribute it to sexual frustration.

"There's not much to tell," he finally answered.

"Everybody has something to tell," she urged, subtly shifting closer to him.

He grew even more tense as she swayed against him, held his gaze with her beautiful, beguiling eyes and pleaded for a response.

"Everybody has likes and dislikes," she said. "Favorite books or TV shows or movies."

When he failed to respond, she continued, undaunted. "I enjoy movies myself, but I'm especially fond of the theater. Have you ever seen the classic *Phantom of the Opera?*"

Kyle froze. His muscles locked and his mind went blank for an instant. *"Phantom of the Opera."* The code for recognizing Sullivan's undercover operative. He'd been waiting for someone in the organization to use that phrase. A phrase no other member of Harold-son's family or staff was likely to use.

He stared at the perfect, pouting lips, wondering if he'd misinterpreted the message. The undercover agent's nickname, Phantom, registered in his brain, but he couldn't reconcile the fact that the beautiful, possibly treacherous woman in his arms was one of the FBI's top operatives.

Haroldson's lover? Sullivan had said Phantom was deep in the organization, but this staggered the mind. He couldn't imagine any agent being dedicated enough or reckless enough to sleep with the enemy. Nor could he imagine the deputy director condoning it, however badly he wanted Haroldson brought to justice.

He had to be missing something.

She gently nudged him into motion, and Kyle automatically took the lead again. He stared into her eyes. Were they glittering with satisfaction, or warning? Was her expression taunting him for his unprofessional reaction?

Her husky voice interrupted his thoughts. "Am I boring you, Tony? You seem to have gone into a trance."

He didn't have to be a genius to realize he'd blown his cover like a raw recruit. At least where she was concerned. Allowing himself to be caught so totally off guard could get him killed. Might still get him killed if he didn't pull it together.

He continued to stare at her, studying the creamy skin of her cheeks, highlighted with a hint of natural blush, the lips that glistened with lipstick as red as her gown.

He silently cursed Sullivan for setting him up to extricate a female agent. His last partner had infiltrated

Haroldson's organization, too, but she hadn't made it out alive. Margie—his partner, best friend and lover. The thought of her made his breath hitch. She'd given her life for the job, and he'd never forgiven himself for not being there to protect her.

Samantha slid her hands to his chest and flexed her fingers against his shirt, her nails scoring him through the lightweight cotton and jarring him back to the present.

"Cat got your tongue?" she whispered.

Her touch lit a fire beneath his skin, making his blood run hotter. Kyle fought the wave of heat and racked his brain for the code Sullivan had given him to verify his own identity. He recalled the answer and recovered some control.

"I don't know nothin' about no phantoms," he declared exactly as he'd been coached. "I don't go for that high-brow stuff."

Her smile widened. She batted her lashes flirtatiously even though her eyes sparkled with keen intelligence. A paradox, to be sure, but could he trust her? Kyle continued to scrutinize every feature of her face, his mind still coming to terms with all he'd heard about Phantom, all he'd learned about Haroldson's fiancée, and what a helluva tangle the whole assignment had just become.

According to his instructions, she was the agent in charge of the rest of the assignment. Once they'd made contact, he'd been ordered to let Phantom orchestrate the escape strategy. He waited, barely breathing, for her to make the next move.

"I like you, Tony. I think I'll have Gregory reassign you as my personal driver."

Her throaty announcement was accompanied by a

seductive thrust of her hips, just as the music came to
an end. But the ploy to tease him backfired. Heat sim-
mered between them; the intimate connection sparked
and crackled. Blood sizzled beneath his skin, and he
knew she felt it, too.

Her brow creased at the undeniable attraction. Annoyance shimmered briefly in her eyes before being
quickly replaced by iron determination, then her more
proper hostess facade.

In any other circumstances, Kyle would have
laughed out loud at the telltale crack in her armor. He
wasn't the only one who'd been caught off guard by a
spark of desire. Maybe in the future she'd be more
careful about teasing a man.

"What do you think, Tony?" she prodded, her tone
edged with impatience. "Want to be my personal
driver?"

"That sounds just fine, ma'am."

"Samantha," she insisted. Then she slipped out of
his arms and strolled off the dance floor.

He watched her closely, appreciating the gentle sway
of her hips as she moved across the room, and wondering if he'd just signed his own death warrant.

One thing was for sure: this assignment would be
coming to an end soon. Adrenaline pumped through
his veins at the knowledge. He'd finally been offered
a real challenge, to get Phantom out of harm's way and
to the FBI's safe house. Sullivan had sworn the evidence she'd collected would be enough to nail Haroldson.

Both prospects spurred his excitement, fueling a
long-suppressed need. He could have done without the
sexual jolt, but he was an expert at tamping down those
flames.

"What'd I tell ya, Tony?" Damon met him as he left the dance floor. Handing him a cold beer, he elaborated. "She's something, ain't she? I'll bet that's the first time you ever held such a classy piece of sugar in your arms. You looked a little starstruck."

Kyle glanced sharply at the other man. So Damon had noticed his momentary confusion. Damn. How many others had witnessed his involuntary reaction? He'd been so distracted that he'd lost objectivity. A good agent had to be observant at all times. Lives depended on it.

Swallowing a long drag of beer, he comforted himself with the fact that he wasn't a field operative anymore. He was a woodcrafter from a sleepy Texas town who'd been dragged back into service. Just a civvie doing a deferred duty. His pride still stung, but he figured he could live with another dent in his ego.

"Haroldson must be crazy to turn her loose on his employees," he finally said, wondering if the slight insult to their boss would be tolerated.

Damon just chuckled.

"He's crazy, all right. If she was my woman, I'd keep her chained to the bed. Preferably in the buff."

Kyle felt a spurt of annoyance at the lewd suggestion, but he quickly stifled it. An explicit, erotic image followed, teasing him with a slender, shapely body all soft and naked and needy in bed. Regardless of her name or game, he wouldn't mind getting more intimate with the body.

For that reason, he avowed sexy Samantha/Phantom off-limits. He prided himself in learning from his mistakes, and the biggest of his life had been getting involved with a female agent. His relationship with Margie had sent up all sorts of red flags, yet he'd arrogantly ignored the warnings. Her death had been an emotional blow he never wanted to repeat.

Foul play or fair, the lovely Phantom had prostituted herself to the scum of the earth. He believed in honor and duty, but not if it meant selling your soul to further your career. Nothing she could do or say would ever erase the facts, and that dropped her desirability to zilch.

Samantha made her way back to Haroldson's side on legs that weren't as steady as she'd have liked. Her heart pounded, her breasts felt full and tight, and her skin was flushed with heat. The intensity of her arousal was unsettling. She didn't appreciate the way her body had come alive in a stranger's arms.

For most of her adult life, she'd existed in sexual limbo, devoid of any burning desire beyond professional duty. She'd met and dated a few men she found attractive, but none who'd made her wild with desire. She'd never been easily aroused, and had resigned herself to the fact that she must somehow be lacking.

The emotional and physical reserve was an advantage to her career, if not her personal life. Now, all of a sudden and at the worst possible time, she'd experienced the hots for a total stranger. It had to be the mental strain and incredible tension of the situation, she decided, shaking her head.

She reached Gregory's side, and he pulled her hand through the crook of his arm. His touch was cold compared to the masculine heat she'd just experienced. She repressed a shiver of revulsion.

A head taller than her, Haroldson was trim and fit, his spine ramrod straight. He had handsome, aristocratic features with dark brown eyes. His personal hairstylist made sure the color of his hair stayed the same dark brown, so that he looked younger than his sixty years.

His expression was affectionate and approving. She gave him a practiced smile that hid her true feelings. It wouldn't do for him to know how much she despised him, from his polished good looks to his ugly black soul. When they'd first met, it was all she could do to keep from recoiling at his touch, but she'd hardened herself to that emotional weakness.

The past few months had been an ongoing nightmare. The only thing that kept her sane was the knowledge that it would be over soon. Haroldson had destroyed her family, and now she had the evidence to prove it.

She forced herself to slip back into the role of fiancée and hostess. She'd made it her life's work to bring him to justice, but the only way to do that had been to get close, really close. It meant drawing on incredible reserves of strength, and it got more difficult each day, but she'd worked too long and hard to fail now.

"What did you think of the new guy?" he asked.

"He seems nice enough. A little lacking in personality, perhaps, but pleasant. Is he a good driver?"

"Nearly as good as Damon."

"In that case, you should have Damon driving for you again. You're on the road more than I am. If the new man is good, I'm sure I'll be safe with him."

Gregory patted her hand. "Your wish is my command," he insisted. "You'll be perfectly safe with Tony. He knows that I'm fanatic about my future wife's welfare."

She smiled, forcing her expression into one of

warmth and gratitude. It was imperative that she keep up appearances. He thought her a well-bred, sophisticated socialite, so that's what she'd become for the past few months.

He'd proposed to her in an effort to garner more respect. For Gregory, image was everything. Respect was a living, breathing entity. He'd spent a lifetime accumulating wealth and power in hopes that it would buy him the respect he so badly craved.

That's why he'd decided to pursue a partnership with one of North Carolina's oldest and most reputable import-export companies. He wasn't satisfied with ruling his own small empire. He wanted to prove his respectability to the whole community.

As a prominent banker, he was welcomed into many social circles but he wanted a foot in the door of the most elite. He'd been advised to marry someone who'd be an asset to his home and social life. That's where she'd stepped into the scene.

He boasted that he was a hardworking man who'd realized the American dream. The story he gave the media was one of rags to riches: a life so dedicated to work that he'd had no time for personal relationships. In reality, his wealth stemmed from a lifetime of carefully coordinated crimes. He owned several offshore banks where he laundered drug money and practiced tax evasion.

But that wasn't why she wanted to bring him down. He had far greater sins to answer for. One was the murder of an undercover FBI agent. Another was the slaughter of a small, law-abiding family. Hers. She had put her life on the line to bring him to justice. And when she did, maybe, just maybe, she could shed a heavy burden of guilt that never seemed to ease.

Another glance at Gregory sent a shiver down her spine. She wondered, yet again, whether he was somehow aware of her double life.

Chapter 2

Three days after the party, Kyle got orders to drive Samantha to a beauty salon in Elizabeth City. He deliberately thought of her by her alias to distance himself from the woman behind the facade. Every time his fantasies drifted toward the feel of her in his arms, he quickly slammed the door on his memory.

She preferred to travel in a Mercedes, and he had no complaints. It handled like a dream, and had plenty of power plus bulletproof windows. He hoped her escape plan didn't include a shoot-out, but he wanted to be prepared for any eventuality.

Rudy, one of Haroldson's most trusted bodyguards, accompanied them. Big and muscular, he looked like a brainless bull moose, but looks were deceiving. He moved faster than a jackrabbit and was nobody's fool. His responsibilities included escorting Samantha into the salon and waiting there while she had her hair styled. Haroldson was notoriously protective of all his possessions, especially his fiancée.

Kyle waited in the car, surveying the area for any sign of other guards on Haroldson's payroll. Security had tightened in the past few days, making him wonder if their assignment had been compromised. He sensed that Samantha would make her move soon. He expected her to enact her plan in the dark of night, not the middle of a bright summer day, but he wouldn't be caught off guard again.

An hour after entering the salon, she exited, looking every inch the pampered socialite. Her jeans were designer tight, accenting rounded hips and long legs. She wore red again, this time a full-sleeved blouse, unbuttoned down the front to display a white knit top that hugged soft, full breasts.

Despite the casual wear, there were diamonds at her throat, on her wrists and fingers. The brilliant sunshine caused them to shoot sparks in every direction. The only difference he noticed in her personal appearance was a fuller hairstyle. As well as a purse that was big enough to pass for a suitcase, she also carried a shopping bag with the salon's name on it.

A ripple of masculine interest spread through Kyle as he watched her slow, graceful movements. He felt a punch in the gut when she smiled at her escort, but he swiftly stifled the reaction.

Rudy followed a few steps behind her. He opened the back door of the car and held it, while she took a seat, filling the car's interior with her unique, expensive scent. Then he closed the door, opened the front passenger door and settled in the seat beside Kyle.

"Where to? Back to the house?" he asked, glancing at Samantha in the rearview mirror.

"I need to go to Anderson's Jewelers and have the safety catch on my bracelet checked. Do you know where it's located?"

Kyle had spent his spare time learning his way around the city. He knew every alley, intersection and parking lot, but not every business.

"What's the address?"

"It's out near the strip mall," offered Rudy.

"The south side of town," she added.

Bingo. So this was it. Her side trip would take them to the edge of the city, close to the freeway interchange. The safe house was to their northwest, but it would be smarter to head south, and then change directions once they were sure they weren't being followed.

Showing no reaction, Kyle nodded and put the car in gear. His muscles tightened, tension slowly coiling in him as he tried to anticipate how she'd neutralize Rudy. The big man wouldn't be easy to handle.

He waited, alert, as she started rustling through the shopping bag.

"Paulo gave me some samples from his exclusive new perfume line," she told them chattily. "I can't decide which one I like best, so I need a masculine opinion."

The high seat backs and headrests prevented the men from having a clear view of her, but they heard the *hiss* of an atomizer. Then her hand reached between the headrests. She put a tissue near Rudy's face and let him inhale the perfume.

"This one's called Ambrosia," she said, shifting the tissue toward Kyle so he could get a whiff before she withdrew it.

He heard her spraying another sample, then another

tissue was held toward Rudy's nose. "Now this one is called Sweet Nectar. It has more of a fruity scent, don't you agree? I'm not sure I want to smell like fruit. What do you think?"

Rudy mumbled a vague reply.

Damn. She was good. Kyle hid a grin as he obediently sniffed at the second sample she held near his face. Haroldson's henchman wouldn't know what hit him when she finally made her move.

They heard the spray of another atomizer, and she was reaching around the seat again. Then she slapped an ether-soaked cloth over Rudy's face, holding it tightly with both hands. He grabbed at her wrists, but she'd locked his head in a vice between her hands and the headrest. The bodyguard struggled briefly before realizing he couldn't break her hold, then he reached for the beeper at his belt.

Kyle grabbed his wrist and held tight until the big man sagged into unconsciousness. Then he hit the window button to let some fresh air into the car so the ether wouldn't affect them.

"So which do you like best?" She continued the charade in case the car was bugged. Then she slithered over the seat and slid between him and Rudy. The action had her body bumping against his, her thigh brushing his shoulder and chest. Kyle steeled himself against the feel of her wiggling form.

He offered a noncommittal grunt in response to her question.

"You guys aren't much help with the perfume preferences," she said on a heavy sigh as she shoved Rudy's limp body closer to the door, maintaining a conversational tone. "I guess I'll leave the choice to Gregory. How about some music?"

Kyle switched on the radio and cranked the volume to cover their conversation.

"What next?" he muttered.

"Anyone tailing us?" Her husky tone had been replaced with a crisp, no-nonsense whisper.

"Damon in a dark green SUV. I can't see who's with him."

"Lose 'em. I want to dump Rudy out of here before the ether wears off."

Considering the bodyguard's size, it wouldn't take more than a few minutes for him to recover. Kyle altered their route and headed for a less congested area of town. Once they'd cleared the heaviest traffic, he had a better view of the car following them. He made a couple of unexpected turns, and Damon started closing the distance between them.

"He's suspicious," she grumbled, dividing her attention between Rudy and the car behind them.

The traffic began to thin out as they reached an industrial park. The area was nearly deserted on Saturday, so Kyle made a sharp turn between two huge warehouses. They were nearing the end of the connecting alley when the SUV came into view again.

For the next few minutes, they wove in and out of alleys, slowly increasing their lead. Then Rudy started to stir.

"Stop in the middle of the next one," said Samantha.

He did as she said, slowing the car enough for her to open the door and nudge Rudy onto the pavement. The big man fell with a *thud* and a grunt. She slammed the door, and Kyle floored the accelerator, peeling rubber, as she settled into the bucket seat.

The plan went like clockwork. They were just pulling out of the alley as Damon was forced to stop for a groggy and stumbling Rudy. The few minutes it took their pursuers to get the extra man into the SUV gave them the time needed to disappear.

Kyle shot out of the complex and turned onto the nearest residential street, and then another, tires squealing. Meeting minimal traffic, he sped up for another few streets, then made a third turn onto a deserted, tree-lined street.

Pulling into the drive of a small ranch-style house, he quickly punched the code of a remote garage door opener. It slid upward, he drove inside, and the door closed to conceal them from the street.

As soon as he'd switched off the ignition, he motioned toward the dusty, nondescript black pickup truck parked next to them in the two-car garage. Samantha grabbed her bags, and they jumped from the car.

"Good plan, Jackson. I was afraid we'd have to elude Gregory's men in his Mercedes."

"No. Too easy for him to track." He'd rented this place to store a getaway vehicle and a few of his personal things. Haroldson would probably track down his car if he had it bugged, but not until they were long gone.

They climbed into the truck. He stripped off his dark shirt, leaving him in a white T-shirt. Then he reached for a baseball cap on the dash, tugged it over his head and hit the ignition.

"Shouldn't we wait a while?"

"Too risky. They've already called for backup, but they won't be looking for a truck with one occupant." He gave her a meaningful glance.

"Got it," she said, sliding to the floor and crouching

out of sight just as Kyle activated the overhead door. He backed the dusty truck from the garage.

Heart racing and adrenaline pumping, he found it hard to control the urge to speed, but he wove back through several residential streets at a sedate pace. As he approached the intersection that led back to the main highway, he spotted the SUV, but it didn't follow as he made the turn.

Within another two miles, they'd reached the freeway ramp leading south. As he paused at the yield sign, he spared a glance for his passenger, and then did a double take. She'd lost the long blond hair, apparently a wig, and now had short, spiky red hair. She'd also shed her blouse for a white knit top and ditched the jewels along with the pampered princess look.

The new look suited her new role.

Their gazes met, and something dangerously sexy arced between them. His muscles clenched as the unwelcome heat curled through his bloodstream. Undercover girl became more fascinating with each layer she revealed.

Her instant frown and the tightening of her jaw convinced him that she didn't appreciate the unexpected attraction.

"Got another ball cap?" she asked, breaking the strained silence. "I'm getting a little cramped down here."

He glanced in the rearview mirror again, then handed her a hat. After donning it, she slowly eased into the passenger seat and fastened her seat belt. Her tone was terse when she spoke.

"Where are we headed?"

"South for a while," he explained, easing into traffic. "Then we'll be turning north toward the safe house in Virginia."

Samantha nodded.

He thought she relaxed a little, but she kept a close watch on the traffic around and behind them for an unexpected tail. After a few minutes of silence, he offered a compliment.

"You handled Rudy like a pro."

Her tone chilled. "I am a pro."

Kyle hid a grin. Touchy. He didn't doubt that the mysterious Phantom was one of the best, but she also had to be insane or inconceivably ambitious to live with a slimeball like Haroldson. What could possibly motivate a beautiful young woman to that extent?

Despite doubts about her mental stability, he was finding her more intriguing by the minute. Which meant, the sooner they parted ways, the better. He didn't want or need involvement with a sexy, lunatic secret agent. He couldn't deny his yearning for uncomplicated feminine companionship, but there was nothing uncomplicated about his current companion.

He'd be glad to have his end of the job finished. A heady sense of freedom rushed through him. In a couple of hours, he could head home to Texas and know he'd done his part in bringing Haroldson to justice. The thought brought a sweet surge of satisfaction.

Samantha withdrew a cell phone from her bag. She punched in a series of numbers. He heard ringing and a pickup. She punched another series of numbers, and then snapped the phone closed.

"Notifying someone?"

"Sullivan. He'll know we're on our way when he gets a coded message from this number."

It pleased him that she had mentioned Sullivan's

name and that the two of them had the operation so
ingeniously coordinated. That meant less chance of
confusion or errors. Fewer risks meant higher achieve-
ment rates.

"So you're the infamous Kyle Tremont?"

He gave her a sharp glance. How had she learned
his name? "You've been in regular contact with Sullivan? Wasn't that risky considering how close Haroldson has you guarded?"

"I haven't talked to him, but I knew he planned to
contact you. He promised me someone who couldn't
be compromised. I've seen your photo in old agency
files and read about a few of your accomplishments. I
don't remember your hair being so dark. Dyed?"

Kyle nodded, a wave of nostalgia tightening his gut.
She was one of them, one of the FBI's elite force of
undercover agents. He'd known a few female officers,
and they had his utmost respect. Margie had worked
twice as hard as a male agent and rarely got the rec-
ognition she deserved. The law-enforcement world was
still a male-dominated profession.

"You shed your blond locks pretty quick. Are you
a natural redhead?"

"No."

She didn't elaborate, which stirred his imagination.
When he realized how curious he was to know more
about her, he abruptly halted the direction of his
thoughts.

She continued. "You earned quite a reputation with
the agency."

"Not all good," he qualified. "I hated the political
games."

"Is that why you quit the agency at the ripe old age
of thirty? You just got fed up with the politics?"

"Partly," he said.

"So what made you decide to come out of retirement for this job? Did Sullivan call in markers or do you have a personal vendetta against Gregory?"

Kyle ground his teeth to keep from growling that it was none of her business. Her questions ticked him off, but he supposed she had a right to ask.

"I don't owe Sullivan any favors."

His passenger wisely didn't pursue the subject. She could believe whatever she wanted, because he didn't plan to offer any details. She didn't need to know about Margie or the guilt that had haunted him for four years.

Margie would have admired Samantha, he thought, his chest going tight. She'd always wanted to do undercover work. When she'd finally gotten her big chance, she'd walked into a trap that had cost her life. The memory made him angry and restless, so he changed the subject.

"Do you have a name besides Phantom or Samantha?" he asked, studying her profile while she stared out the windshield. "Is that your real name or is it a top-level security secret?"

She hesitated, glancing his way and then turning her attention forward. It was the first time she'd acted tentative about anything. Kyle found himself wanting her to trust him, yet annoyed that it mattered.

He'd almost given up on an answer when she finally responded. "You can call me Rianna, if you'd like."

Rianna. He liked it. It sounded soft and feminine. A little inconsistent with what he knew about her, yet appealing.

"That's a pretty name, but unusual."

She hesitated another instant, then added, "My given

name is Marianna, but I've always shortened it in one form or another.''

Not a giant leap of faith, but a baby step. He didn't expect much more. He knew how hard it was for an undercover agent to trust anyone after months of being constantly on guard, when a slip of the tongue could blow your cover and end your life. He didn't know how long Rianna had been hiding behind a phony name and background, but he knew it would take her a while to unwind.

Neither of them was inclined to make small talk, so conversation came to a halt. As the miles passed by, they watched the passing scenery, kept an eye on the traffic behind them and gradually relaxed.

Kyle grew increasingly aware of her scent, the warmth radiating from her body and even the soft, steady sound of her breathing. His senses absorbed everything about her in an intense, disturbing fashion, even while he argued the idiocy of the reaction. He comforted himself with the thought that their forced alliance wouldn't last much longer.

It took them a little over two hours to reach the state border and cross from North Carolina into Virginia. Their destination, a single-story house on the outskirts of Emporia, was easily found. Surrounded by several large bushes and evergreen trees, it sat apart from any neighboring houses.

Kyle turned into the drive, pulled to a stop near the front porch and shut off the engine.

Tension hiked upward a few degrees as they faced a new and unknown territory. He and Rianna both studied their surroundings for a long time before considering it safe to get out of the truck. He reached for her bags, but she halted him.

"Leave them for now."

His gaze held hers for the first time since they'd left Elizabeth City. More tension flashed between them, complicated by a touch of suspicion. Her wary expression didn't surprise him. She wasn't prepared to trust anyone or anything right now. He nodded, understanding the reaction, and climbed from the truck.

Rianna let him lead the way to the front porch. He found the key where he'd been told to look and preceded her inside the house, then stopped.

"Stay put a minute," he said, reaching for the gun he'd tucked in the waistband of his jeans.

She ignored the command and accompanied him as he searched the house, checking each room thoroughly and making sure they were alone.

"Everything looks okay," he said a few minutes later as he slowly replaced his gun. "Sullivan should have gotten your message by now. He'll have a couple of agents here to guard the place in an hour or so. They'll be coming from D.C., so it shouldn't take them long."

"You're not staying?"

Their gazes met, hers slightly accusing. He ignored a brief pang of guilt.

"My part of the plan was to get you out of Haroldson's estate and to this safe house. That's all I agreed to do."

"So you're ready to disappear?"

The antagonism in her tone had him clenching his jaw. "A week of playing lackey to Haroldson is more than any man should have to take," he argued grimly. "As soon as your bodyguards show up, I'm outta here."

Rianna snorted indelicately. "Meantime, I'm

starved,'' she said. ''I think I'll see what kind of food we have stocked.''

His annoyance vanished at the thought of food. It had been a long time since breakfast, and a meal now would help him avoid making extra stops on his way home. He decided not to argue.

''Sounds good.''

Kyle followed her to the kitchen and watched while she rummaged through the refrigerator. He admired the way her jeans molded the feminine curves of her hips, thighs and long legs. A man would have to be emasculate not to notice how well she was put together, but that's as far as his interest went.

He quickly redirected his attention. Moving to the window, he surveyed the backyard for as far as he could see. The house was secluded; there was no sign of neighbors and everything was quiet.

''Are you eating?'' asked Rianna.

''Sure.''

He turned back and helped her get the food on the table. They put together some sandwiches, opened a bag of potato chips and ate in silence. Kyle studied her as he chewed, familiarizing himself with her new punk look. It suited her oval face and delicate features as well as the seductive blonde image. He wasn't sure which he preferred.

It seemed Phantom was a chameleon, as well.

''Do you mind if I ask what you do now that you're not with the agency any longer? Do you still live and work in D.C.?''

He'd never been comfortable discussing his personal life, but he didn't see the harm in small talk. ''I moved out west a few years ago.''

''You still work in law enforcement?''

"No, I'm just a private citizen who minds his own business."

Her brow creased in a frown, and he realized how censorious his comment sounded. She abruptly stopped asking questions and grew quiet, which should have pleased him, but perversely didn't. They finished their meal in silence, and then worked together to clean the kitchen.

After they had taken turns in the bathroom, he switched on the TV in the living room while Rianna paced around the house, checking the contents of cupboards and closets.

She had just stopped her restless prowling and joined him, when a knock at the front door startled them.

"Stay out of sight," he told her, heading toward the front of the house while she headed toward the back.

A glance through the peephole showed two familiar faces, Dan Hoskins and Ted Blaine, both experienced agents he recognized from his days at the bureau. Tucking his gun back in his jeans, he opened the door. They shook hands and exchanged greetings, then he lead the way back to the kitchen.

They found it empty. Kyle glanced at the door, then toward the window, annoyed and confused until noises from the bathroom helped him pinpoint Rianna's location. He heard the toilet flush, some clinking of the toilet tank, and then she called to him for assistance.

"Kyle, could you help me again? This toilet still isn't flushing right."

He had no idea what she was talking about, but he decided to find out. "You guys help yourselves to some lunch. I'll be right back," he said, walking down the short hallway to the bathroom.

To his surprise, his reluctant charge was slipping

backward out the narrow window. She spared him a
fierce glance, jerked her head toward the front of the
house and disappeared.

He flushed the toilet again, stalling for time and
making more noise to cover her actions. Then he followed her out the window, feetfirst. It was a tight
squeeze, and he muffled a grunt as he hit the ground.
By the time he'd rounded the corner of the house, she
was flattening the tires of the agency's sedan with a
pocketknife.

"Let's go," she said in a terse whisper, climbing
into the truck and quietly closing the door.

"What the hell?" Kyle demanded, but he didn't hesitate to follow her lead. All he could do was trust her
instincts until he knew what had spooked her.

"The guy who called you a renegade retiree."

"Blaine?"

"I don't know his name, but I recognized his voice.
I've heard it on Gregory's private phone."

"Sonofabitch!" Kyle's hoarse oath echoed in the
cab as he hit the ignition. His first instinct was to con-
front Blaine; to beat some answers out of the rotten,
low-down traitor. Personal need warred with common
sense. As much as he wanted to grill the other man for
answers, he had to consider Rianna's safety first.

There was nothing lower than a cop on the take.
How long had Blaine been on Haroldson's payroll?
How long had the man been dirty? Long enough to
have orchestrated Margie's disappearance and death?
Kyle ground his teeth in frustration, clenching the
steering wheel and slamming the truck into gear while
mentally vowing to get some long-overdue answers.

They heard shouts behind them as they sped down
the street, but lost sight of the house when they turned

at the next intersection. They were both too busy checking for other threats to worry about the stranded agents.

Sure enough, the green SUV pulled from the curb as soon as they hit the connecting street. Kyle pushed the accelerator to the floor.

"Damon and Rudy."

"I saw them," she said grimly, pulling a semiautomatic out of her bag. It looked big and heavy in her small palm, but she handled it skillfully, checking the load and flipping the safety.

When they turned onto a nearly deserted, straight stretch of road, she opened the passenger window. "Swerve to the right."

"And give them a clear shot at you? Hell, no."

"Give me a clear shot at them."

"You're a better marksman?"

"I'm good. Now, swerve."

Kyle did as she asked, veering the truck to the right so she could have a straight shot at the SUV gaining on them. He heard her squeeze off four successive shots, then she swung back into the cab and stayed low.

There was no return fire.

He steadied the truck again, changed lanes, then glanced in the rearview mirror. One of her shots had shattered the windshield of the SUV, but Damon hadn't slowed his pursuit. Kyle knew how skilled he was at the wheel.

"Haroldson wants you alive."

"For a while, at least," she agreed. "He always has a master plan and his own agenda."

They hit the green light at the next intersection and turned into heavy, two-lane traffic. Another look in the mirror showed Damon running a red light, but steam was starting to roll from beneath the hood of the SUV.

"Did you puncture their radiator?"

"That's where I aimed," she said, lifting her head long enough to check behind them. "I figured it would be the fastest way to disable the car."

"You're right."

Within a few minutes, the tailing vehicle was engulfed in a cloud of steam.

"They'll have to slow down now."

Kyle took advantage of the pursuing vehicle's problems and wove in and out of rush-hour traffic until he'd put a good distance between them and other pursuers. After traveling several more miles, he thought they'd probably lost the SUV. He turned his attention to his passenger again.

"What now?"

"I have a contingency plan."

"Glad to hear it." His tone and expression were harsh. "Care to fill me in?"

Rianna didn't respond right away, but she eased herself upright and faced forward, pulling her seat belt around her. "If we get on the interstate and head south, I know a small town where we can stop over and switch vehicles again."

"Another safe house?"

Her lips tightened. "At this point, I'm not trusting my life to the agency. I'll find my own safe place and then make new arrangements with Sullivan."

"And what do you figure my role will be in your alternative plan?" he grumbled, his hopes of a speedy return to Texas fading fast.

Tension sizzled in the silence that followed. They both knew he didn't want any further involvement, but he'd promised Sullivan to keep her safe until she had adequate protection. He didn't make idle promises, and this one had just taken on a whole new perspective.

"That's up to you," she said. "You can drop me off in Hendersonville or you can accompany me to my destination."

"Which is?"

"Ultimately, Kentucky."

"What's in Kentucky?"

"It's not what's there, but who and what *aren't* there."

"Haroldson and the strong arms of his organization?"

"Right."

Kyle had little alternative but to follow her plan of action. It grated that he'd been so close to making his solitary getaway, but he couldn't just dump her alongside the road. He'd have to stick with her until alternative plans could be coordinated with Sullivan.

Reining his frustration, he focused his thoughts on Blaine, mentally reexamining every aspect of the agent's participation in Margie's last assignment. Not for the first time, he wished he knew more about what went wrong that day. The lack of details was a constant thorn in his side.

They drove through the late afternoon with minimal conversation, each lost in thought. Much to his annoyance, Kyle grew increasingly aware of his sexy, enigmatic companion. He became attuned to every subtle move she made; his nerves jangling when any part of her shifted closer to him.

They passed a car with a kid mushing his face against the window, and Rianna chuckled softly. The sound punched him in the gut, making him feel things that weren't safe to feel.

Despite his fundamental longing for a woman, he knew better than to get physically or emotionally tangled with this one. She was trouble with a capital *T*. She represented everything he knew he should avoid—federal bureaucracy, undercover activities and Gregory Haroldson's criminal dealings.

And she was another man's lover. The circumstances were strange, to be sure, but that still made her off-limits. He tried not to focus on her quiet, undemanding presence or wonder what she was thinking and feeling.

To keep his thoughts off his hormones and his companion, Kyle replayed the events of the day over and over in his mind.

He wondered if Hoskins was as dirty as Blaine. They'd seemed surprised to see him at the safe house, so Sullivan must have kept his involvement a secret.

How much of the agency's security had been compromised? Blaine had been an agent for years. How much money did it take to buy a man's soul? How much to make him betray his comrades or sign death warrants for co-workers?

How widespread was the corruption? He wanted a few words with Sullivan, but didn't want to make contact through the agency. He'd wait and call his home number later. It was long past the time for some answers.

Frustrated with his own thoughts, Kyle's attention turned to Rianna. She lifted a hand to rub the back of her neck, the first small indication of weariness. She had to be exhausted, yet she hadn't uttered a word of complaint.

In profile, she looked deceptively young and innocent. Her lashes had a pretty, feminine sweep of curl. The soft curve of her cheek made her look almost delicate when you couldn't see the stubborn set of her chin or the iron determination in her eyes.

She was a paradox, to be sure, one that challenged him more than any woman had done for several years now. Off-limits, he reminded himself sternly, turning his gaze back to the road.

Chapter 3

They reached Hendersonville just as the sun was setting. Rianna gave him directions to a small, private storage unit. Once there, she produced a key to unlock one of the garage stalls. He lifted the overhead door and triggered an automatic light switch. They did a quick check of the space, and then she climbed into a small car and started the engine. Kyle stepped aside while she backed out of the narrow space.

Now it was decision time. He could either send her on her way alone or break his self-made promise not to get more deeply involved. Even as he cursed his own streak of chivalry, he knew there really wasn't any choice. Call him a chauvinist and a fool, but he couldn't desert her while she was being hunted by the likes of Haroldson. Despite his disapproval of her methods, she was trying to bring the other man to justice.

As soon as she'd cleared the building, he hopped

into the truck and drove it into the storage unit. After grabbing their bags, he pulled the door back down and secured it. He'd planned to drive the rental back to Texas, but he'd have to take care of it later. Now it could be recognized.

When Rianna approached to relock the storage unit, their gazes tangled and awareness crackled between them. Her expression softened with gratitude. The slight chink in her tough-guy armor stabbed him with unreasonable pleasure, but he stiffened himself against the emotion.

"I promised Sullivan I'd stick with you until you were safe," he said, making light of his decision.

She nodded, accepting without comment. When she moved close enough to grab her bag from him, every hair on his body reacted to her warmth and scent. He clenched his fists to keep from touching her, and searched for something to break the tension.

Turning, he took a good look at their new transportation. Then he swore. "Pink? You expect us to hide in a pink car?"

"It's mauve," she insisted. "And it's perfect. Who'd ever believe we were on the run in a mauve economy car?"

He grumbled, but couldn't argue the logic. Neither Haroldson nor the FBI would be searching for a compact sedan.

"I'll drive," she said as she headed for the driver's side and stowed her bag in the back seat. "You have to be getting tired, and I'm used to driving in the mountains."

He didn't argue, just moved to the passenger side and threw his bag in beside hers. The space was cramped, the bucket seat small, but he slid it back as far as it would go and strapped himself in. She did the same, and they were on their way again.

Hendersonville was little more than a crossroads with a couple of streetlights. Traffic was minimal. They found a convenience store, made use of the bathrooms and filled a thermos with coffee.

Rianna bought a variety of supplies, making him wonder where she planned to take them. Another safe house? A rental? The home of a friend or family member? He hoped it was someplace he could safely leave her and head back to Texas with a clear conscience.

She stood by while he used a pay phone to call Sullivan's private number. There was no answer, so he left a short, terse message on the answering machine: "Blaine's your mole. We're on the run, but we lost our tail and Phantom is okay."

Though rarely comfortable with another driver, Kyle climbed into the passenger seat, and Rianna drove back onto the highway. He remained tense for the first few miles, but soon realized that she could handle the car with the same ease she did everything else. Was there no end to her talents? He relaxed a little, deciding to pry some information out of his cohort.

"Sullivan told me you were in deep, but he didn't hint at how deep. My reaction to your identity could have gotten us both killed."

"Rookie mistake," she taunted.

The barb stung, but Kyle knew he deserved it. "Retiree mistake," he corrected sharply.

"Whatever."

Her voice held a teasing note, making him wonder if superwoman might have a sense of humor.

"How'd you manage a marriage proposal?"

She hesitated briefly, but then explained. "Gregory

wants legitimacy and the image of a normal, healthy lifestyle. I played the part of an impoverished but highly eligible socialite with a pedigreed background.''

''The perfect bait?''

Her features tightened mutinously, making him realize how disparaging his tone had sounded.

''It worked.''

The succinct reply held a touch of hurt and made him feel like a heel. He cursed himself for not being more diplomatic. She'd been under a tremendous amount of strain, yet it bugged him to think of any woman offering herself as bait to a man with so few scruples. Her deception would be all the more personal and galling to an egomaniac like Haroldson.

Was she a total rebel? Some power-hungry female who enjoyed living on the edge? A lunatic who thrived on danger? Hadn't she realized she'd be flirting with certain death if he ever got his hands on her again?

A mental image of Haroldson touching her made Kyle grind his teeth. He didn't want his protective instincts roused, yet she kept getting under his skin.

He had to ask. ''Why did you move in with the guy?''

''I had to have unlimited access to the estate without him watching my every move. I tried for weeks while we were dating, but finally decided there was no other way.''

Kyle made an effort to sound curious rather than accusing. ''So why you? Why would any woman put herself in such a dangerous, compromising situation? Just to prove yourself with the agency?''

The silence stretched until he thought he'd pushed too far. Finally, she responded in a tight voice.

''We all have our crosses to bear, Tremont. I have

my reasons, but they have nothing to do with proving myself or advancing my career. I can't be bought, and I'm not motivated by greed or glory, so that's all you need to know.''

He cursed the fact that her passionate response only served to make him more curious.

"How about a change of subject," he suggested.

"Okay by me," said Rianna. "Why don't you tell me about yourself. Where's home for you now? That's not classified information, is it?"

"Far from it." He remembered how well-informed Sullivan had seemed about his current lifestyle. "I live in Texas, not too far from El Paso."

The small bit of casually supplied personal information caused a slight relaxing of her rigid posture. Her shoulders sagged a little, and he wondered how she was handling the unrelenting stress.

"I've always been curious about Texas but I've never been there," she said, then asked tentatively, "Is that where you grew up?"

"I grew up everywhere. I was a military brat."

The urge to see her at ease had him offering details about his private life. "Both my folks were Air Force officers. We moved around a lot, but I spent my early years and most of my summer vacations with Granddad Tremont in Texas. He was a craftsman. I inherited his knack for working with wood, and his home. I moved back there when I retired from Uncle Sam's employ."

His granddad had also been a decorated Second World War veteran. From the time Kyle was old enough to listen, he'd heard tales of the war, the cost of freedom, and a man's duty to serve his country. They'd watched old movies and cheered when justice triumphed over evil. He'd hung on every word of his granddad's lectures, vowing to live by the same high principles. He'd taken it all to heart—but it had nearly cost him his soul.

"Did your parents retire to Texas, too?" she asked.

Her tone sounded wistful, and he studied her profile. What did her family think of her career? Maybe she didn't have anyone. That might explain why she'd been willing to risk her life for a job.

"Dad died about four years ago, and Mom remarried. She and her new husband are stationed in Germany right now."

"Sounds like she's really dedicated to the service."

"Yep, that's how I was raised. Everything's right or wrong, black or white, with no in-betweens. That's why I got fed up with the FBI."

"Too many shades of gray?" she asked in a tone that suggested she really understood.

"Yeah, way too much gray."

They were quiet for a few miles, each lost in thought, and then she spoke again. "Donald said you left because you lost a partner and blamed the agency. Is that true?"

Kyle stared out the window, watching the scenery flash past as his memories fixed on Margie. She'd been more than a partner. So much more. Impotent rage still churned in him when he dwelled on the unfairness of her death.

"Margie went undercover while I was on leave for Dad's funeral. She went in alone, but with standard backup from the agency. She understood the risks."

Logically, Kyle knew he might not have been able to save Margie, but emotionally, he still felt responsible for not being there for his lover and friend. After years of trying, he'd finally realized he couldn't be content until the man responsible for her death was brought to justice.

Rianna broached her next question softly and cautiously. "The records suggest that she might have turned bad."

"That's a filthy lie!" Kyle snarled, making her jump and go tense again.

He tempered his next words, but they still quivered with underlying fury. "That's what pisses me off the most. An agent gives her life for her country, and what does she get in return? A damn blight on her record? Rumors that she was on the take? That's why I hate the freakin' politics. The FBI lost an agent, so they try to save face by suggesting she's the one at fault!"

A thick silence fell in the car, but the unbridled strength of his emotion pulsed between them, intimately binding them in its intensity. Kyle took a deep breath, uncurled the fingers he'd fisted, and forced himself to relax again. It was futile to give in to the long-simmering frustration.

His loss of control unnerved him and made him realize he was bone-tired. Otherwise, he wouldn't be wasting time and energy on useless venting.

Rianna spared him a glance. "That's the gray part you hated so much?" she asked quietly.

"Enough to make me call it quits."

She nodded, and something about the small, supportive action clutched at his gut. It had been a long time since anyone had really cared or understood his feelings. He needed to shut her out before she had a chance to undermine all his good intentions.

"I think I'll take a nap."

Rianna kept her attention on the winding, mountainous road, but stayed alert to every move and sound her passenger made. Tremont reclined his seat, stretched out his legs and crossed his arms over his chest. Finally, he settled his long, lean body in the tight confines.

The tension in the car eased along with him, like the cleansed calm after a storm.

"Sure you're all right to drive?" he asked, tipping the bill of his hat over his face.

"Positive," she said, still too wired to relax. "I rested earlier."

"It's been thirty-six hours for me. I could use some shut-eye."

"I imagine you could. Will it bother you if I listen to cassettes?" Music was one of her greatest passions, probably because it was a continual, no-risk pleasure that warded off loneliness. "Our radio reception won't be very reliable for a while."

"Music doesn't bother me unless it's that rap stuff."

"No rap or heavy metal, I promise."

"Glad to hear it."

There was just a hint of teasing in his tone. It surprised and warmed her, so she responded in kind. "Then, go to sleep. If I get drowsy, I'll wake you."

"Do that."

His comment sounded more like a command. Rianna shook her head, but didn't respond. Men, she thought, they always want to be the ones in charge. She recognized and could tolerate the attitude as long as it suited her purposes.

A half-hour outside of Hendersonville, she heard his breathing turn slow and steady. The sound of his soft snoring was strangely comforting, which worried her.

It made her wonder at her own reactions to the FBI legend.

She'd been shocked by her physical response during the brief moments she'd spent in his arms on the dance floor. She'd held her own emotions under rigid control for so long that she'd begun to feel like a zombie. The sting of attraction had been so alien that she almost hadn't recognized it. Now that she had, it had become an unwelcome complication.

Being cooped up in their current tight quarters stirred her senses again. Heat radiated from Tremont, enveloping her. His sheer size and stature tugged at something elementally feminine in her, something she couldn't quite analyze.

Maybe a compact car wasn't such a good idea, but she hadn't given a thought to prospective passengers when she'd bought it. She'd always been something of a recluse, and her lifestyle didn't allow much time for men or long-term relationships. Her greatest strength was the ability to function in any given situation while maintaining emotional distance—protected in her own insular little world.

So why was she having such a strong reaction to this man?

His service record had fascinated her from the beginning—dedication to duty coupled with a renegade personality. He'd been both praised and damned by his peers, but his devotion to job and country had never been in doubt. The fact that Donald Sullivan trusted him implicitly was testimony enough to his integrity.

That didn't mean she fully trusted him. She'd been alone for too many years, fiercely independent, working toward one goal with steadfast, obsessive determination.

Did she find Tremont attractive because he represented an end to her self-imposed isolation? The light at the end of the long, dark tunnel? Or because he represented all that she'd given up to accomplish her goal?

She was twenty-eight and had bypassed the usual coming-of-age flirtations—the dating games and variety of partners most people took for granted. She'd never trusted any man with her heart or her body, and didn't plan to start now.

As a teenager, she'd had a serious crush on an upperclassman. Her family had been in the witness protection program because her dad testified against his former boss, Gregory Haroldson. They had feared their location had been compromised and wanted to move, but she'd begged to stay for the high school prom. It had cost her mom, dad and brother their lives. Since then, she hadn't let anyone get too close, nor had she let anyone interfere with her quest for justice.

To Gregory, she'd been a possession, a means to an end, just another collector's item. She'd told him she wouldn't have sex until they were married. It had been a condition of their engagement, and he'd agreed. He had other women, but they were more than welcome to his amorous advances.

Men like Tremont—handsome, smart and reeking of sex appeal—usually had a bevy of women vying for attention. He could even have a wife or lover or significant other. She glanced at his left hand. He didn't wear a wedding ring, but that could be for any number of reasons. Why hadn't she thought to ask when he'd been talking about his family?

It annoyed her that she'd missed the opportunity to pry some more. He'd been unexpectedly forthcoming

about his parents, his dead partner, and his grievance
with the agency. His exhaustion had probably contrib-
uted to his candor, but it wouldn't hurt to give it another try when he woke.

Rianna gazed into the unending darkness of the
mountains, broken only by her headlights and an infre-
quent passing car. For the most part, the skies were
cloudy with random glimpses of a star-studded sky.
The slivered moon did little to illuminate the winding,
ascending road.

She didn't mind the darkness. Her thoughts were
equally dark. Over the next couple hours, she reviewed
the past six months in her mind—the conversations
she'd overheard, the records she'd unearthed and the
security she'd breached. With her testimony, they could
put Gregory Haroldson behind bars for the rest of his
life.

It had taken every ounce of courage she possessed
and a strength born of necessity to carry out the assignment. Pretending to accept his proposal and moving into his home had taken nerves of steel, but she'd
sworn to make him pay for destroying her family. That
pledge had seen her through the worst of it.

In her mind's eye, she projected the image of her
mother, dad and brother. It was a vision that comforted
her in times of extreme stress. They'd been the axis of
her world until Gregory Haroldson had ordered their
deaths. If she'd been a little stronger, a little wiser, or
a better person, she could have prevented what happened. The knowledge ate at her like a disease. The
only way she knew to counteract the guilt was to make
Haroldson pay for his crimes.

No jury in the country would fault her for the engagement deception. Not once they heard the whole

truth. She and Donald were banking on that fact. There was no way their undercover operation could be labeled entrapment. Haroldson's corruption dated back too many years to afford him that defense.

We have him. We have him. We have him. The litany ran through her mind like the constant spinning of the car's wheels. *We have him. We have him.*

When Rianna realized she was becoming mesmerized by the sound of her thoughts, she reached out and touched Tremont's arm. Heat and muscle. The warmth of another human being. The comfort it offered unnerved her a little because it was so unexpected. It was a pleasure she rarely enjoyed with anyone but her adoptive parents. The contact soothed her, subduing the painful turbulence of her memories.

Her passenger stirred, tilted his hat back and glanced up at her. She watched him in her peripheral vision, feeling her own body come awake with tingling alertness as he uncoiled his arms and straightened in his seat.

They'd reached the peak of the mountains, shrouded in late-night fog. She dimmed her lights to cut through the haze, and then spoke to Tremont.

"There's a roadside rest area a few miles ahead. I thought we might get out, take a break and stretch our legs. I'm starting to get numb."

"Sounds good," he mumbled.

His voice was so low and husky and incredibly sexy that it snapped her senses to alertness. A tremor of reaction tingled along her spine. It was a quick fix to her lethargy.

"Any of that coffee left?"

"About a cupful, but it's only lukewarm." She

handed him the thermos, then wrapped her fingers around the steering wheel.

"I want to try and reach Donald again if the pay phone's working at the rest area." She'd already decided to call, but threw out the comment for conversation's sake.

"I don't mind waking him in the middle of the night. I hope he's sound asleep. I owe him one." After all, Sullivan had called him at four a.m. to request his help.

"Even if someone traces the call, there's no way to pinpoint our exact location," she expanded. "Once we clear the mountains, we could go in any direction."

"Do you have a specific destination in Kentucky or is it just an unlikely spot for someone to find?"

Rianna deliberated, but then decided to trust him even further. "I'm familiar with the Cumberland Lake area, so that's where I'm headed."

"A resort lake?"

"Miles and miles of man-made lake. It's all buried in a deep valley between jagged, boulder-lined hills topped with a thick wall of evergreen trees."

"A nice place to get lost?"

"That's what I'm hoping." She wanted nothing more than to disappear, to fade into the background after months of constantly being in the spotlight and on display.

The rest area was nearly deserted as they pulled to a stop in the parking lot. Rianna climbed from the car, grabbed her bag and headed for the rest room with Tremont close beside her. They parted ways inside the utilitarian concrete structure.

She used the toilet in the women's room, splashed water on her face at the sink, brushed her teeth and restored some order to her hair. It took a while, but she managed to tame some of the spiky tufts of the punk hairstyle. The result wasn't very flattering, but it was a whole lot less noticeable. The last thing she wanted to do at this point was draw attention to herself.

Feeling more human, she rejoined Tremont near the pay phone. He'd freshened up, too. His hair was damp and a shade lighter, evidence of his attempt to wash out the dye. He'd shaved off the mustache, which drastically changed his looks. Rianna's admiring gaze traced the smooth curve of his lips. A firm, sexy mouth, she thought, before quickly redirecting her thoughts.

He'd already dialed the number and was greeting Sullivan when she stepped closer. Their gazes met, and she was taken aback by the crystal-clear blue of his eyes. He'd shed the dark contacts, altering his looks even more. The clarity of his steady gaze caused her to shiver. It felt as though he could see right into her soul, and she knew it wasn't a very pure place.

Tremont turned the receiver so that they could both hear.

"I got your earlier message," said Sullivan. "But Blaine's dead. Killed by Hoskins. According to him, Blaine pulled a weapon and tried to shoot at you when you left the safe house. They scuffled over the gun and Blaine was fatally shot."

Kyle and Rianna exchanged frowning glances, neither sure what the latest twist could mean.

"You'll be watching Hoskins?"

"For sure, and we'll do some serious checking on Blaine's record. I'll personally interrogate everyone he's worked with."

"When are you having Haroldson arrested?" asked Tremont.

"First thing Monday morning, but there's a glitch.

His lawyers will demand he be released on bail, and
there's a good chance we won't be able to keep him
long.''

"What about his flight risk?'' insisted Rianna, her
heart sinking at the word *glitch.* Gregory wouldn't want
to leave his little empire or the U.S., but once he realized how damning the evidence was against him, he
had the money and connections to disappear. "I
thought once we had him jailed, we could keep him
there indefinitely.''

"I did, too, but as soon as you disappeared today,
he made a public announcement that you'd been kidnapped. He's conducting a media circus, featuring himself as the devastated fiancé who's bravely coping with
a great tragedy.''

The information had Kyle and her staring at each
other in disbelief.

"So that's his master plan,'' she whispered. "He
wants the world to believe I've been kidnapped. That
way he gains a lot of sympathy without having to deal
with me himself.''

"He also gains the means to get us permanently out
of his hair,'' Tremont added grimly. "That's why it
was so easy. He's been playing us all along. If we turn
up dead, he'll have an alibi, someone to blame for your
murder. Then, if I'm conveniently killed by one of his
men, the murder will seem justified.''

"You're probably right, but that won't help him
against the indictment,'' said Sullivan.

"He's not aware of that yet,'' she reminded. "We're
still the only ones with access to that information,
aren't we?''

"Yes, and that has to stay a secret until I get the
arrest and search warrants. If not, there's a risk of him

fleeing. Meanwhile, he's playing the media for all it's worth. I'll have to publicly acknowledge your identity or risk having a judge release him on bail," explained Sullivan.

"How bad's the risk for Phantom if you expose her identity?" Tremont asked. "Haroldson must know she's a federal agent by now."

"Even if he does, it won't keep him from putting a contract out on both of you. Her disappearance threatens her standing with the bureau, since we don't have her in protective custody. If I can't verify her whereabouts, that leaves us without a witness who can support the indictment."

"You're suggesting we come to D.C.?"

"Are you staying with her?"

"I said I would."

Tremont's tone was getting harsher by the minute. Rianna studied his fierce expression and wondered what concerned him most—the risk to her safety, the risk of weakening their case or the thought of prolonging his own involvement. It worried her that she was beginning to care about his motives.

Sullivan took his time answering. "No. I'll swear I know where she's being held. You two disappear for a few days until we see how this is going to play out. Keep in touch with me through this number. If I'm forced to produce a witness, we'll worry about additional security then."

They ended the call and Tremont replaced the receiver. Only then did Rianna realize how close the two of them were standing. Her right shoulder and arm were pressed against his chest, the heat of him permeating the thin layers of her clothes. It seemed so natural, yet disturbing. She had an unprecedented urge to press closer, and that wouldn't do at all.

Once they stepped apart, she felt a chill and shivered.

"You're cold. We need to get back in the car," he insisted, and surprised her by wrapping an arm around her as they moved toward the parking lot.

Her first instinct was to shift from the warmth of his touch. She didn't want to seem weak or needy, but she was cold and tired and trying to ward off an emotional collapse. She'd been warned by bureau psychologists about a dramatic letdown after an undercover assignment.

Maybe she'd be wise to accept a little impersonal support. Just as long as it remained impersonal. So far, she and the renegade retiree were making a pretty good team.

Kyle offered to drive, but Rianna insisted that she'd rather continue until they were through the mountains. She drove while he caught a few more hours of rest. Then they exchanged places, but she still wasn't able to sleep.

They shared a comfortable silence, passing the time listening to music and studying the darkness beyond the windows of the car. Rianna had picked up a map at the rest area, so she navigated them through southern Kentucky. By daybreak, they were nearing their destination.

"Where are we heading now?"

"I think Somerset is one of the largest towns in the lake area," she said. "It's not too big, but it offers the basics. If I remember correctly, there are several docks, and check-in times at the marinas are about the same as most hotels."

"Marina?"

"I'm planning to rent a houseboat if there's one available," she explained, glancing at him and wondering if he was going to bail out on her now. "The lake is huge, so you can disappear for days at a time without anyone checking up on you."

"You can actually stay out on the water?"

"It's been years since I was there, but I remember cruising around until we needed to refuel. At night, we'd set the anchor near the shoreline and stay put. Either way, you avoid contact with civilization."

"You've vacationed there in the past?"

"Once, a long time ago." The thought made her melancholy, but she tried to shrug it off. "How about you? Are you interested in staying or do you want to head on home? I don't see any possible way I can be traced now, so you don't need to feel obligated."

"I said I'll stick with you until Sullivan makes other arrangements."

"What about your family? Do you need to get home to a wife or kids or a partner of some sort?"

Tremont threw her a rakish grin. "'Partner of some sort'?"

"Partner, as in significant other or anyone who expects you home soon."

"Fishing for more details about my private life?"

The man really could be maddening. Rianna gritted her teeth. "I think it's important that I know the basics," she insisted.

"What you see is what you get," he finally said. "I don't have to account to anyone for my whereabouts. Not even Sullivan, since I already honored my promise to help you escape Haroldson's estate."

"No regular job? Are you one of those independently wealthy men who risks his life for kicks?"

Tremont's gruff chuckle rippled over Rianna like a sweet, sexy melody. Her heart thudded uncharacteristically. She scolded herself for the foolish reaction, realizing how desperately she needed sleep.

"I'm not rich, that's for sure. Unless you count the fact that I own my own little place. I'm self-employed. Nothing out of the ordinary."

No way would Rianna ever consider this man ordinary. He might prefer to think of himself that way, but she couldn't.

"Do you know anything about boating or fishing?"

"Not much."

Neither did she, but they were intelligent, resourceful adults. They could learn.

Conversation lagged as they covered the last hundred miles of their journey. The sun was rising behind them as they reached the outskirts of Somerset.

Their first stop was another convenience store and refueling station. They filled the gas tank and bought souvenir T-shirts. Then they freshened up with a change of shirts to cut the risk of being recognized. They'd drastically changed their looks since leaving the coast, but it didn't hurt to cover every angle.

Next they found a small roadside restaurant and took their time over breakfast and coffee. When the place started to get crowded, they drove into town. Rianna asked Tremont to stop at the local post office.

He stayed in the car while she rented a post office box and bought two padded envelopes. In one, she mailed herself extra cash and a fake driver's license at her personal P.O. box, knowing the post office was the safest place to hide it in case of another emergency.

She used the second envelope to mail all her jewelry to her adoptive aunt Margaret's address in Maine. It was a risk to mail anything so valuable, but the necklace, bracelet and rings were all gifts from Gregory. They held no sentimental value. If she ever got a chance to sell them, she'd make good use of the money, but she wouldn't be destitute if the jewelry got damaged or lost.

They spent the next couple of hours driving around the town and familiarizing themselves with the area. When the stores finally opened, they purchased additional clothing, more groceries and a few other necessities.

Rianna found a brochure with information on boat rentals, so she called several marinas until she found one with a recent cancellation. After learning that a houseboat was available immediately, they headed for the lake.

''What's the name of the place?'' asked Tremont.

''It's called Beaver Creek Resort, and it's near Monticello. There are several marinas with docks and fuel stations, but the only one with an availability is Beaver Creek. This is the height of their tourist season, so we got lucky. I think they said they have one good-size houseboat for rent.''

''What's good-size?''

She showed him the picture in the brochure. ''There are several types, each in a different price range with different amenities and the capacity to sleep a different number of people. I guess ours is over sixty feet long.

''According to the brochure, it features a galley with a gas stove, refrigerator, running water, generator, central heat, AC, microwave, electric lights, deck furniture, gas grill, swimming ladder, power steering, and a sliding board off the top deck.''

Tremont whistled softly. "Sounds like a small yacht, and looks like it must be top of the line."

"Nope, top of the line is a lot bigger, sleeps more people and costs more."

He shot a glance at her. "Which brings up the question of how we're going to pay for this rental. I don't carry around that sort of cash, we can't charge it to Uncle Sam, and we sure can't use plastic."

"I have several thousand dollars' worth of cash with me," she told him, earning herself another, longer, sharper look. "When I moved in with Gregory, he insisted on giving me an allowance and buying me designer clothes. I've been hoarding the money and even selling a few designer gowns."

His laugh wasn't pleasant. "So your lover is paying for our little hideout."

Rianna managed to keep her temper reined, but just barely. "He and all the people he's swindled out of money, including Uncle Sam," she returned succinctly.

The reminder of Haroldson cranked the tension between them again, so they grew silent, speaking only about directions. The road that led to the marina was sharply winding, and they drove downhill at a forty-five-degree angle for more than fifteen minutes before Tremont complained.

"You're sure this dock isn't in China?" he asked, as they kept going downward, mile after mile, in the seemingly endless spiral of a roller coaster.

"I told you the lake was carved out of solid rock. It takes a while to get down to the water."

She hoped the high rock walls would be an added barrier between them and Gregory's far-reaching network of criminals.

Chapter 4

The marina came into view just as she finished explaining, and she caught her breath at the sight. There were boats in all sizes and shapes. Some were moored while others were coming or going on the water. The whole place was bigger, more modern and a lot more commercial than she remembered, but the overall beauty still held her in awe.

Her heart thudded heavily in her chest as emotion ballooned inside her. She could visualize her parents holding hands, laughing and teasing while her brother chased after them, always skipping and chattering. There hadn't been many happy, carefree times for her family, but they'd shared one wonderful week here.

The precious memories brought a lump to her throat and a rush of rare tears to her eyes. She swiftly blinked them away as Tremont parked the car.

He turned more fully toward her, and Rianna knew

he sensed a change in her. His demeanor underwent a subtle change, too.

She clenched her teeth and turned her head to avoid his probing gaze. She hated feeling so emotionally fragile. The memories were private and cherished, so she kept them carefully guarded in her heart.

"You okay?"

She wanted to allay his concern by responding in a crisp, no-nonsense fashion, but her voice failed her. To cover her awkwardness and give herself more time, she grabbed her bag and searched for a wallet. Once she'd found it, she opened the door and climbed from the car without a word.

Tremont got out of the car and followed her toward the marina. "Better tell me how we're registering," he insisted.

That had her pausing to regroup. She swallowed the last of her silly tears and turned to him. "Think we can get by with separate names and IDs?"

"Sure, it's common practice these days. We don't have to pretend we're married. We can just be lovers," he explained, his eyes challenging her to refute.

The suggestion sent a shiver of awareness over her, but she humphed, pretending the idea was too annoying to consider.

Since she was handling the money, the houseboat was rented under the alias Donna Elise Simons. The normal check-in time wasn't until three p.m., but due to the last-minute cancellation, their boat was ready to be boarded.

They left the car in a hillside parking area and hauled everything onto the boat. A dock attendant gave them a quick tour and basic watercraft instructions. Shortly after noon, they were casting off and making their way toward less congested waters.

Rianna quickly accustomed herself to the hum of the engine and its steady vibration as they glided over water as smooth as glass. The sun shone brightly, making everything sparkle with a freshness that soothed her nerves within minutes.

Tremont settled behind the steering wheel, just inside the combined living room and kitchen area. He wore a short-sleeved blue T-shirt that made his pale eyes look darker and deeper. She alternately admired the beauty all around them and his physique. His shoulders and chest were broad, the strength in his arms apparent as he easily maneuvered the big boat.

His thighs, encased in tight, worn jeans, also contracted with solid muscle. The rest of him was lean and just as appealing. She silently admonished herself for mental drooling and tried to concentrate on the water.

"It really is gorgeous here, isn't it."

"Yeah, and probably one of the last places Haroldson would expect his high-society lover to hide."

"I'm not really, you know," she insisted. At his searching glance, she bit back the words she'd almost blurted in self-defense. Knowing it was safer to let him believe she had the morals of an alley cat, she rephrased her response. "I'm not really a high-society type."

"If you say so," he muttered.

All of a sudden, Rianna felt the strength drain from her limbs. Exhaustion overtook her with unexpected speed and force. She stared blankly at the water, then Tremont.

"Something wrong?" he asked, concern creasing his brows.

"I'm tired."

His laugh sounded more like an abrupt bark. "I'll bet you are. You've been running on nothing but caffeine and nerves for days. Ready to crash?"

"Yes" was all she said. Then she moved toward the sleeping compartments, her feet and limbs feeling like lead. She fell across the first bed she found and dropped off to sleep within seconds.

Kyle spent the rest of the afternoon learning his way around the lake. A map hung above the steering compartment that displayed the overall size and shape of the waterways, but he needed to get his bearings.

Over one hundred miles long, the lake had winding waterways that covered sixty-three thousand surface acres with twelve hundred miles of wooded shoreline.

The entire shoreline was dotted with sandy-beach coves surrounded by twelve-foot-high, boulder-strewn banks. They'd been told that boaters could drop anchor in the coves to picnic, swim or fish during the day and to sleep at night. He liked the idea of being able to find their own private niche.

When hunger and thirst eventually had him stirring from his perch at the helm, he let the boat idle and went to check on Rianna. He found her sprawled, face-down, on one of the double beds. She was down for the count.

The total abandon of her position made his stomach muscles clench. Her slim, pale arms were flung, spread-eagle, across the mattress. A wedge of creamy skin was exposed at the small of her back. Her jeans-clad rump was slightly elevated, and he had an insane urge to crawl into bed and wake her with caresses.

"Whoa, boy."

He issued the soft, urgent warning to his body as blood began to pool in his groin. An unexpected arousal burgeoned against the zipper of his jeans, pulsing to life and sucking the air from his lungs.

Heat crept up his neck as he fought the temptation to slide his body over hers and wake her with greedy hands and mouth. He wanted to explore every dip and curve of her feminine form, and lose himself in her softness. The urge was so primitive and shocking in its force that he shuddered. What the hell had prompted the sudden, intense hunger?

It was the ultimate in stupidity—a risk neither of them could afford. Kyle shook his head to rid it of lecherous thoughts. As tempting as he found his sexy partner, he couldn't afford to get any more involved with her.

Instead, he slowly slipped her shoes off her feet and eased her more fully onto the bed. She didn't so much as flinch, testimony to how soundly she slept.

He soothed himself with a cold beer, and then another, as he tried to shove Rianna from his thoughts. She'd probably sleep through the night, so he was left to his own devices. Normally, he preferred his own company, but her proximity kept him restless.

After slapping together a couple of sandwiches, he washed the meal down with a third beer, his personal limit, then went back to the helm. He found a cove to anchor in for the evening, where he could do some fishing. By the time dark had fallen, he was ready to call it a night himself.

He secured the front and back doors, and then carried his bag to the small compartment opposite the one Rianna had chosen. The bathroom was smaller than a

phone booth, but Kyle showered, brushed his teeth and
donned a pair of clean sweatpants.

After steeling himself to check on his companion
again, he grabbed a blanket and covered her lightly,
then quickly retreated to his own full-size bunk. He
didn't expect to drop off easily, but the soothing sounds
of the country night and gentle rocking of the boat soon
lulled him to sleep.

The rising sun coaxed him out of bed the next morning, and Kyle quickly checked on Rianna. She was still
fast asleep, but she'd apparently been up during the
night. She'd shed her jeans and crawled under the
covers, leaving only one long, bare leg exposed. The
sight of the slim calf and thigh caused his blood pressure to rise, so he swiftly shifted his attention to her
upper body.

His eyes widened a little as he studied her head. The
red hair, obviously another a wig, was gone, tossed
aside like lifeless vermin. In its place was a cap of light
brown hair that parted down the middle and curved
across her cheek. It looked as soft and shiny as corn
silk.

Something inside him went soft, too, as he glimpsed
yet another layer of the woman. Both the elegant
blonde and the brassy redhead had been fascinating,
but easily abandoned. Now Rianna looked sweet and
natural and so desirable that he had to fight another
fierce shaft of desire.

The real woman was slowly being revealed, like a
flower opening its petals, and each new revelation in-
trigued him more. He wondered if her personality
would undergo a similar transformation. She'd be ex-
periencing an emotional letdown, so it would be a

while before she even recognized her own personality. Not much use in speculating.

With that thought, he moved into the kitchen area and brewed a pot of coffee. While it was perking, he watched the early sunshine glisten on the water. A light morning haze hung on the air, but there were no other watercraft to disturb the view—just soothing, unblemished isolation.

It looked as though they'd have another warm, calm day on the lake. Maybe he'd swim in lieu of his usual run. Or maybe he'd check out paths along the upper bank. It was always good to have an escape route, however safe and isolated the location.

When the coffee was ready, he filled a cup and turned toward the narrow hallway. Rianna materialized in the doorway and they collided with a soft *thud*. She fell against him like a limp rag, her face buried against his shoulder. Kyle clutched her close with his left arm while he set down his cup. Then he tentatively rested his right hand at the small of her back.

Instead of moving out of his grasp, she burrowed closer, like a sleepy child. Her arms encircled his waist, a ring of fire that seared him. The feminine warmth and scent of her made his pulse leap wildly, and his body come to full sexual alert.

"Coffee. I smell coffee," she mumbled innocently against his shirt.

The feel of her mouth moving against him, even through the cloth, made his muscles clench with excitement. Her breasts pressed into his chest, branding him with erotic fire.

He closed his eyes, savoring the sensual pull, then took a deep breath. He wanted to lock her tightly in his arms, ravage her mouth with his own until he'd forced her to wake up and accept the consequences of her actions.

Desire raged through him as Rianna drifted back to sleep in his arms. She obviously wasn't a morning person. Kyle clenched his jaws in frustration. He considered carrying her back to bed and having his way with her. As much as the idea appealed, he wasn't the sort of man who took advantage of women, especially vulnerable ones.

That didn't mean he couldn't enjoy having her close, he thought.

He tightened his grip, pulling her body snug against his own. A moan escaped him at the exquisite feel. Rianna moaned, too, then suddenly went rigid in his arms. Kyle grinned as her head jerked backward, and she stared at him in sleepy confusion.

He slowly loosened his hold on her. She eased her grip on his midsection, allowing her enough room to splay her hands on his chest. More heat.

"What?" she muttered huskily.

"You came in search of coffee and ran into me."

"You're—" she began, then cleared the huskiness from her throat and licked her lips.

Kyle wanted to suck each glistening lip between his own and then devour her whole mouth. The need was so strong that he had to fight for control. How the hell had he gotten so needy?

"You're very hard," she finally managed to say.

And getting harder with each breath he took. "It's a morning thing," he supplied.

Her brows puckered, lashes sweeping upward as the drowsiness cleared from her eyes. As she came more fully awake, she began to withdraw.

"A guy thing," she clarified for them both, then stepped out of his reach.

"Yeah."

"I'm sorry if I made it harder."

Kyle watched a rosy blush steal up her neck and over her cheeks as she realized what she'd just suggested. The flustered color made her all the more alluring.

"I'll survive," he teased, then decided to give them both a break from the escalating tension. "I just need some coffee."

"Coffee," Rianna parroted.

He reached for his cup, sipped it to see if it was still warm, and then downed the whole thing. Maybe the caffeine would knock some strength back into his knees.

After she filled her own cup, she refilled his.

"Thanks," he said. "I was just heading outside to welcome the morning. Care to join me?"

"Sure," she said, then preceded him through the narrow hallway between their sleeping compartments.

Kyle reached around her to unlock the door, held it open while she passed through, and closed it behind them.

"I want to go up on the deck," she said, turning toward the ladder.

The roof of the houseboat doubled as a sundeck with chairs, tables and an attached sliding board for swimmers. Kyle took another sweeping glance around the area, noting that all was still quiet. He followed Rianna up the ladder, feeling his body respond to the sight of her shapely bottom, clad only in gym shorts that left a whole lot of leg exposed. Smooth, sleek legs that could feed a man's fantasies.

He forced himself to concentrate on security. "You

can't get too comfortable up here. We're as close to being sitting ducks as we can get."

"I suppose," she said, easing herself onto a lounge chair and stretching out her legs. "But it's just about the most perfect spot anyone could want to be."

Kyle had to agree. He settled into the chair opposite her and allowed himself to relax a little. The sun was beginning to sparkle on the water, burning off the morning haze. The waves were gently lapping at the boat in a peaceful rocking motion. Birds were singing as gulls squalled and dove for breakfast. The morning was clear and bright with a slight nip in the air.

"Are you warm enough?"

"I'm chilly, but it's invigorating, not uncomfortable."

He nodded, feeling the same. The sun would warm them before too long. It had already cleared the horizon and was moving upward like a brilliant ball of fire.

They sat in silence for a while, enjoying their coffee and absorbing the peaceful beauty around them. Neither of them had known much peace these past few weeks, so it seemed a rare and welcome pleasure.

"I guess I really conked out on you last night. You didn't have any problems, did you?"

"Not a thing. I explored a little, had something to eat and did some fishing."

"Did you see anything out of the ordinary?"

"Just a few other boats and some late-night fishermen. Nothing suspicious or threatening."

Rianna sighed, resting her head against the back of the chair and closing her eyes. "Sounds wonderfully dull."

"It was," agreed Kyle, gazing out over the water.

Margie would have loved it here.

The image of his former partner slipped into his thoughts, unbidden. She'd had dark, wild curls that were always out of control. Her eyes had been dark brown, too.

Normally, the memories were too painful, so Kyle kept them buried where they couldn't rub him raw with bitterness and frustration. But Margie had been on his mind a lot during this assignment, a result of working with another female operative.

She'd tackled life head-on, as if it were a great, unending adventure. Born and raised in the city, she'd loved doing anything outdoors, exploring new places and tackling new challenges, but it was that same daring personality that had cost her life.

Even the good memories made his jaw clench and his chest tight. For a long time, he'd been mad as hell at her for risking her life and abandoning him. Now he just felt sad at the loss of her life. Sad, and determined that Haroldson should pay.

Shaking his head to dismiss the images, he turned his attention back to Rianna. She could easily distract a man from troubling thoughts. He studied the smooth curve of her cheeks and noticed how perfectly her hair framed her face.

"I'm guessing that's your natural hair."

She reached up to tuck the ends behind her ears. "This is the real thing, and what a relief to be rid of those awful wigs."

"I'll bet. I'm sure glad to be rid of the mustache. It itched like hell."

"And contacts," they chorused, sharing a grin.

Kyle stared into her lovely, smiling eyes for a moment. Their natural color was a mixture of green and gray. It surprised him to realize how much pleasure he derived from just her smile. It warmed him.

The temperature cooled when she averted her gaze.

He watched as a frown marred her features, and suddenly wished for the power to keep her safe and smiling. He wanted to destroy anything that threatened her, to eliminate anything that might motivate her to put her life at risk. The depth of the emotion made him edgy and restless.

"How long do you think we'll be able to stay here?" she asked, obviously sensing a need to distract him.

"A few days. Maybe through next weekend. I'm betting Sullivan will want you in D.C. the following week, at the latest."

She nodded and closed her eyes again. Kyle couldn't seem to drag his gaze away from her. He knew it was dangerous to let his attraction escalate, yet he couldn't stem the increasing desire to know what made her tick.

Neither could he ignore the surge of impotent fury he felt every time he thought of her engagement to Haroldson—living in his home, accepting his touch, being intimate with a man twice her age.

How could she do it? How could she sell herself in such an obscene manner? What would make an intelligent, capable woman take on such a compromising assignment? She'd hinted at a deeper reason than ambition, so what could it be? A family vendetta?

He'd only known her a few days and the questions were eating him alive. He wanted answers, yet knew better than to ask. Even if she'd be willing supply answers, he wasn't sure he could handle the whole truth. Better to guard against caring too much. All that had ever gotten him was more pain and disillusionment.

"I'm starving," Rianna announced, breaking into

his grim thoughts. "Since you made the coffee, I'll cook breakfast. Any preference?"

"I'm not particular, but I'm hungry."

"Bacon, eggs and toast?"

"Sounds great."

He watched her rise from the chair and walk across the deck. Her smooth, supple movements had his body stirring in interest again, hungry for more than food. He clamped down hard on the desire and spent the next few minutes trying to convince himself that self-denial would make him a better man.

They pulled up anchor after breakfast, and Rianna took the helm for a couple of hours. There really wasn't much driving involved, she mused, just a gentle steering as the big boat chugged across the water.

Tremont had taken a seat on the small front deck, so her attention shifted back and forth between the lake and him. The temperature had climbed to eighty already. He'd replaced his T-shirt and sweats with a pair of gym shorts. The rest of him was gloriously, tantalizingly naked.

A fine sheen of sweat made his bronze skin shimmer in the sunlight. Every time he moved a muscle, the ropelike flexing sent a frisson of sensation through Rianna. She didn't suppose a woman would ever get tired of looking at his tight, flat stomach or his equally tight rear end.

What she didn't dare do was get too excited about his great body. As much as she'd like to explore every inch of it, she knew it would be a monumental mistake. Her assignment for the agency was far from finished. Even if she survived to testify against Gregory—which the odds were against—the trial and appeals could go on for years. She had no business getting involved with anyone.

That didn't mean she couldn't do a little daydreaming about the hunk she'd hooked up with, she thought with a grin. Would he be an impatient lover? Or the slow, thorough sort? Did he like partners who were wild and uninhibited, or shy and innocent? She didn't have any personal experience, but that didn't mean she was totally ignorant about sex. A person could learn a lot through the media these days. Movies, television shows and books were pretty explicit.

Tremont stirred her feminine curiosity more than any man she'd ever met, yet she knew any interest he showed in her would be strictly physical. He wore his emotional detachment like a Mylar vest, shielding his heart.

He chose that minute to reenter the cabin, and Rianna felt a blush rising up her neck. She hoped he didn't have a clue what had prompted her flush.

He offered a convenient excuse. "It's getting a little warm in here, isn't it."

She jumped on it. "Yes, I was just thinking we might want to turn on the AC during the heat of the day."

He moved to the controls and turned on the central air. "I'll set it low enough that it doesn't get cold— just not too hot."

She mumbled her agreement and then turned her attention to the lake again. Tremont stepped behind her, and she was enveloped in the musky male scent of him. He radiated as much heat as the sun, raising her temperature even more. It was all she could do not to fan herself.

As they traversed the main waterway, the traffic was

heavier, with ski boats and Jet Skis zipping around on all sides of them. The boat rocked in the rough wake, and he braced himself with hands on her chair. Even the casual brush of his fingers seared her, and she mentally admonished herself to get a grip.

"How about finding us another place to drop anchor. A place with some natural steps or handholds up the embankment would be nice. I'd like to scout around the area this side of the lake. Maybe have a run if I can find a smooth enough path up there."

Rianna steered around the next jutting of land, then another before turning into an uninhabited cove with a boulder-lined bank. She cut the engine and let their boat drift as close to shore as possible.

"The brochure mentions cottages and other rental properties, so I'd think you could find a decent path somewhere near the shoreline," she said.

"I'll try. Are you a jogger?"

"No, but after you're done exploring, I'd like to swim for a while. I'm used to a good daily workout, and I'm getting stiff just sitting so much," she said.

Once she'd shut off the engine, Tremont stepped away, and she drew a calmer breath. He lowered the anchor, and then grabbed a pair of running shoes.

"Keep your gun handy while I'm gone. I won't be more than an hour. If you even suspect trouble, get off the boat."

"I'll be careful. If I need to escape, I'll follow you onto shore and then stay as close as possible until you get back."

"Okay."

They both moved to the front deck, and he dove into the water. Once he surfaced, she handed him his shoes. She noticed socks were tucked in one and a small handgun in the other. He held the shoes over his head as he waded the last few feet to shore. She watched until he'd climbed the steep bank and disappeared into the trees.

Her emotions were mixed about her sexy bodyguard. There was no denying the physical attraction. Though neither of them spoke about it or acted on it, it kept intensifying. It wouldn't be smart to let her increasing desire fog her judgment. There was so much more at stake than personal satisfaction.

She wanted to trust him, yet she'd been trained to consider every angle, the potential risk in every situation. What if Donald Sullivan was wrong about Tremont's reliability? What did she really know about him? Even though his service record was impressive, he'd retired under less than favorable conditions.

What if both sides had enlisted him to keep her under surveillance? Where did his loyalties lie? What if he'd just headed for the nearest pay phone to contact the men who wanted her dead?

Hating the paranoia that had been a part of her life for so long, Rianna shook her head in disgust. She'd have to wait and watch Tremont until she could decide whether or not to trust him. Right now, being with him held more appeal than being alone. She was so tired of being alone.

Thoughts of the loneliness brought memories of her family and their vacation on a similar houseboat. Her brother, Jimmy, had been so full of energy and enthusiasm. He'd wanted to investigate every nook and cranny, to learn how everything worked. He'd wanted to fish and swim and steer the boat. He'd asked a million questions that her parents had patiently answered.

Jimmy had called her Rianna instead of her given

name, Marianna. It had been too much of a mouthful for him, so he'd created the nickname. Tremont was the first person she'd mentioned it to in nearly a decade.

She couldn't say why she'd shared it with him, except that she'd grown sick and tired of aliases. Once this case was over, she vowed to find a new line of work: one where she never had to assume another name and identity. With Gregory out of the way, it might finally be possible.

Deciding it was a good time to take stock of the clothing she'd bought, she dragged out shopping bags and sorted through the hastily purchased collection. In addition to a few pairs of shorts and tops, she'd chosen four bikinis, two matching navy-blue ones and two neon-green ones. She set them aside and stashed most of the other clothes into the drawers under her bed.

Her biggest purchase had been panties. She took fourteen pairs of them, plus the bikinis, and moved back into the kitchen. After getting herself a can of soda, she settled down to sew, pausing every few minutes to check for unexpected guests.

Nearly an hour later, she heard Tremont shouting at her from the beach. She went onto the deck and waited until he'd swum close enough to toss his shoes onto the boat. Then she gave him a hand to board.

"Have a nice run?" she asked.

"Yeah. The path's a little rough, but it felt good. Any problems?"

"Nary a one," she said. "I saw a few boats pass by on the main waterway, but nothing came close."

"Good. Ready to swim?"

"Almost. I have some sewing to finish. Then I'll be ready."

"Sewing?" he asked, following her back inside the cabin. He glanced toward the table. "Have an underwear explosion while I was gone?"

Rianna gave him a grin. "No, I'm just practicing an old trick my mother taught me."

"And what's that?"

"Well," she explained as she went back to work, "you buy two matching pairs of underwear, then you cut part of the front panel out of one and sew it to the front panel of its mate. That makes a neat little pocket that can be sealed with thin strips of Velcro."

"For hiding something?"

"For hiding a small plastic pouch with cash, an ID, and, in my case, the key to a post office box."

"Nice, neat little package?"

"I never go anywhere without one."

"Even to swim?"

"Even to swim. That's why I bought matching bikinis. The plastic protects everything, so the shower's about the only place I go without my backup supplies."

"Clever. Your mother taught you this?"

"Yes, and it's a trick that's saved me on several occasions."

"I imagine it has," he said.

Conscious of his scrutiny, she lifted her gaze from her handiwork. Tremont had a strange expression on his face. It almost looked like compassion.

"Why are you staring?"

"I'm curious. I know parents teach their kids survival tactics, but why in the hell would your mother teach you something like that? What ever happened to the basics, like putting overzealous boyfriends in their place or protecting yourself against would-be muggers?"

Rianna dropped her gaze again. "My dad taught me that kind of stuff. Mom just expanded on the teachings."

"Why?"

"What do you mean?" she asked, but knew exactly what he meant. How many mothers taught their children strange survival tricks? Hers had done so out of necessity.

"Why did she think you'd need that sort of security?"

"We moved a lot when I was younger."

"So did we, but not without a chance to collect our stuff first. Why would you move with no more security than money tucked in underwear? Were you running from someone or something?"

Rianna debated telling him the whole truth. Instinct told her to trust him, yet it didn't come easily. She held his gaze for a few minutes, and then returned her attention to her work.

"Don't!" He ground the word out harshly, surprising her into looking directly at him again.

"Don't what?" she asked lightly.

"Don't shut me out. Just give me the basics. I can deal with whatever you have to say, and I know how to keep a secret."

Something about the intensity of his demand made her heart stutter. Did he really care? Why? His tone suggested more than idle curiosity, but what? Rianna found herself telling him a little about her childhood.

"When I was twelve, my family got moved into a witness protection program, but we never felt safe. As soon as we'd get comfortable, the location would be compromised and we'd have to move. My parents taught us to be prepared."

"Witness protection? I know about it from the agency's end, but I never gave much thought to living that way. How could your location be jeopardized that often?"

"I don't know." Having finished her project, she gathered up the panties, tossing the ruined ones into the trash. "I was just a kid, so I didn't know all the specifics—just what my parents told me."

"Which agency was in charge of your relocation? Sounds like someone screwed up royally and kept putting your family in danger. Who do you blame for a breakdown in the system?"

She considered his questions as she put her panties away with the rest of her things. He didn't need to know that the FBI had failed her family. Or that she and Donald still didn't know who the informant had been. Blaine had been with the agency for years, so maybe he was the key to learning more.

"I don't know all the answers. I wish I did, but I don't," she said. Having already donned the navy-blue bikini, she headed to the rear of the boat.

Tremont followed, but she ignored him and opened the door to the back deck. "I'm going to swim now," she said, then dove cleanly over the side.

End of conversation.

Chapter 5

Rianna swam for a while, and then did a little sun-bathing. She tanned easily but hadn't been exposed to much sun lately, so she wanted to be careful not to overdo it. After coating herself with a liberal amount of sunscreen, she stretched out in a lounge chair on the upper deck of the boat.

Tremont stood near the railing with a collection of fishing gear scattered around him. She decided to lie on her stomach, but turned her head so that she could admire his casting techniques. Every hard line of his body was aesthetically pleasing.

She couldn't help remembering how solid he'd felt when she'd latched on to him this morning. Even the memory of his reaction heated her blood hotter than the sun baked her skin.

It had been so long since anyone had held her, tightly and securely. Just held her. Without pretense, without making demands she couldn't accept.

He'd wanted her this morning. At least, his body had hungered for hers. The thought thrilled a very private, feminine part of her. She found him wildly attractive and was pleased that he reciprocated the feeling, even if neither of them planned to act on it. It still gave her ego a much-needed boost, a warm, fuzzy feeling to hug to herself.

Gregory hadn't wanted her in a physical sense. He'd had plenty of women willing to satisfy his carnal desires. He'd been openly affectionate in public, but very impersonal in private. The setup had suited her needs, yet it had kept her isolated. She'd had no one she could trust or be comfortable with for months.

Tremont had to be applauded for not trying to take advantage of their forced intimacy. She hadn't known whether his legendary honor extended to personal relationships. She supposed it did, yet she had an insane urge to entice him beyond his control.

What would it take to make him lose control? What kind of woman would it take to make a man like him forget everything but raw, primitive need? Did such a woman exist? Was she stupid to even speculate? Probably. She'd never been the type to stir men to unbridled passion.

Deciding her backside had been exposed long enough, Rianna turned to offer her front to the sun. Tremont had fussed about her staying on deck too long, but it felt as close to heaven as she'd ever known.

Gregory, Sullivan, the agency and its moles were far, far away while she basked on her tiny island of freedom. She tilted a visor over her eyes, but managed to keep Tremont in full view. She loved watching the play of muscles in his arms and shoulders as he swung the fishing pole to cast out his line. His subdued but obvious strength fascinated her.

The midday sun soon had every inch of her skin tingling from prolonged exposure. Flesh that had been cooled by the water was now sizzling. Heat penetrated her bikini top to tighten her nipples, spreading the nerve-titillating sensation throughout her body. Watching her hunky companion increased her arousal, so she shut her eyes and tried to get a rein on her wayward libido.

Dozing and unaware of the passing time, she continued to rest until a shadow fell over her body. At the same time, she felt the gentle splash of something cool on her neck. It sizzled on her overheated flesh. Peeking from beneath the visor, she glared at Tremont. He stood beside her chaise, dribbling bottled water on her sun-drenched skin.

It felt like a liquid caress against her bare flesh, so cool and sensual that her breasts grew full and tight. For that reason only, she gasped and glared at him. He returned her gaze with an unrepentant and totally wicked grin.

"Time's up."

"Uh-uh, I'm not on a schedule."

"Oh, yeah, you are. You've had enough sun and enough exposure for one day. It's not safe to stay out here too long."

"Go away. You're just mad because you can't catch any fish."

"What makes you think that?"

She couldn't confess to having watched his every move, so she improvised. "I haven't heard any of those triumphant male whoops," she drawled. "I think they're a must for you macho types."

"Macho, huh? What if I'm just a kind, sensitive guy who throws the fish back in the water?"

Rianna rolled her eyes in disbelief, and then she returned his grin. In that instant of teasing, something hot and electric flashed between them. So hot that her muscles tensed and her breath got caught in her throat.

Tremont's eyes grew hooded, his features a taut mask as he stared down at her. She licked her lips, feeling wary, yet wildly excited by the fierce hunger throbbing between them. She needed to diffuse the situation before it erupted into passion, yet the look in his eyes held her mesmerized.

"If you're going to waste your water, dribble some into my mouth," she said, never imagining that the simple action could take on the impetus of sexual foreplay.

He did as she asked, watching her with an unblinking concentration as she swallowed, then lapped the excess off her lips. The unbridled flash of excitement in his eyes caused her breathing to grow shallow. Her heart banged against her chest as every nerve ending in her body quivered with excitement.

Closing her eyes against the ferocity of desire in his, she struggled to regain control of her rampaging pulse. Counting to ten and practicing her deep-breathing technique seemed the most practical course of action. At least, until he began to paint her body with the remaining water.

She felt the cooling stream of liquid start at her fingertips, run up her arms, across her chest and then down the other arm. Her skin sizzled, the cool water on her hot flesh causing a potent reaction in every cell of her body.

Next, he bathed her left foot, letting the water tickle

over her toes and then zigzag its way up her calf to her thigh. She felt its pooling coolness on her stomach, where he painted a slow, leisurely pattern of water that caused her breathing to falter and her muscles to contract.

Her right leg got equal treatment, from toes to thigh, then the water settled in her naval. Rianna was coming apart at the seams. The erotic bath made her breasts swell against the confines of the bikini top, her nipples aching for attention.

She didn't think she could get any more aroused, until Tremont aimed the water directly onto those rigid peaks. He slowly and painstakingly saturated each nipple through the cloth until her nerves sung with tension and she felt like launching herself off the chaise.

Her sharply indrawn breath signaled the devastating impact his caresses were having on her self-control.

"Kyle!" The exclamation was a tangle of shock, reprimand and excitement. His first name slipped out, inadvertently destroying another small barrier between them.

"I'm cooling you off."

The words were simple, but his husky tone conveyed a more primitive message. His voice was thick with wanting. He wanted her. Maybe as much as she wanted him. Rianna dragged in a breath and opened her eyes, leveling her gaze at his body. He stood so close that his arousal was directly in her line of view. It bulged beneath the thin fabric of his shorts, signaling his own undeniable hunger.

She knew she should close her eyes and block out the sight, but her body wasn't obeying the frantic mental commands. This man had the power to make her forget all her carefully formed plans. Feeling suddenly overwhelmed and out of her league, her panicked brain searched for a way to shatter the escalating tension.

"I think I'll take a swim. That should cool me." She intended to make a firm announcement, but the words came out all low and shaky. Clearing her throat, she tried again. "Maybe we both better take a dip."

Kyle took a step backward and offered her his hand, his gaze never wavering from hers. The blue in his eyes had gone dark and hazy with need, but he allowed her some space. She slipped her hand in his and let him draw her to her feet. The touch of skin on skin lit more fires along her nerves. Another minute of contact and she'd disintegrate into a pile of ashes.

"Race you?" Her challenge lacked spirit, coming out all confused and breathy.

"Not until I get a drink of that water," he said on a low growl, pulling her tight against him and taking her mouth with savage hunger.

He tossed the empty water bottle aside and clutched her head with both hands as he ground his mouth onto hers. The force of his kiss left Rianna helpless to respond or withdraw, until he gradually eased the pressure. Then she opened her mouth and welcomed his tongue with abandon, stroking and sucking until she drew a moan from deep in his throat.

Her hands clutched at his waist, the feel of the taut, warm skin making her eager for closer contact. He continued to cradle her head, devouring her mouth, while she strained to fit their bodies more snugly together. The rigid pressure of his arousal against her lower body made her insides quiver. Her legs began to tremble, and soon his strength was all that kept her upright.

Kyle finally lifted his mouth, allowing them to gulp in air, and then he nibbled at her lips while she fought to regain some control. Her desire for him was too strong, frighteningly so. She'd never wanted a man as much as she wanted him, and that scared the hell out of her.

Desire warred with common sense, but then he captured her mouth for another long, deep kiss. He coaxed her tongue into his mouth and sucked deeply. She felt the pull of it deep in the pit of her stomach. Moaning and rocking against him, she felt herself falling off a dangerous precipice and fought to pull herself back from the edge.

"Kyle, please!" she whispered against his hard mouth, unclear of what she begged for most.

"Tell me you're protected," he insisted gruffly, grasping her hips, lifting her and pulling her legs around his waist.

The action brought his arousal to the juncture of her thighs, and she gasped at the exquisite feel. So close. The satisfaction she craved was so close, his body straining and throbbing against her. She rocked herself against him and then swallowed his groan in another ravishing kiss.

"Protection," he repeated, while his fingers dug into her flesh and pulled her still closer.

She took birth control pills. A female agent in a potentially dangerous situation had to protect herself against the possibility of sexual assault. But she couldn't get the words past the lump in her throat. She wanted him, ached for him, yet something kept her from making the final commitment.

"No!" She almost screamed the word.

Kyle jerked his head back as though she'd slapped him. She felt every one of his long fingers pressing into her skin as his features underwent a frightening transformation. Rianna watched in horror as contempt replaced the passion in his eyes.

"Forget yourself for a while?" he snarled in a soft, dangerous tone that sent a shiver over her. "Or are you as skilled at teasing as you are at everything else? Another day, another conquest? Is that how you operate?"

For just an instant, she felt a shiver of fear. Kyle's demeanor had changed in the space of a heartbeat. The drastic change shook her, and then it made her sick with shame.

She shouldn't have screamed, but her instinct had been to protect them both. He believed her capable of selling herself, body and soul. It only proved how little they really knew each other. Succumbing to passion would satisfy a temporary urge, but ultimately make their situation worse.

She tried to pull out of his grasp, but he wouldn't let her go. Instead, he swung her into his arms. Stifling the desire to scream, she clung as he moved across the deck.

"Hold your breath," he commanded harshly.

The next thing she knew, they were catapulting down the sliding board. They hit the water hard and sank so deep that she nearly panicked. Quickly disentangling herself from his arms, she fought her way to the surface and dragged in a much-needed breath of air.

He swiftly put some distance between them, swimming toward the shore with strong, sure strokes. Rianna watched him, her heart heavy. What must he think of her? And why did it matter so much? He'd been equally guilty in the explosion of passion, but *she* felt like a fool and a phony.

After dragging in a few long breaths, she floated in

the water until she'd recovered her composure. When he started swimming back toward the boat, she climbed from the water and headed straight for the shower.

Once she'd finished, Kyle took a turn, and she made them a light lunch. They ate in silence, each having withdrawn into a protective shell. Then he spent the next couple of hours boating around the lake while she watched a movie on the VCR. Despite their separate pastimes, each was acutely aware of the other's proximity.

Toward late afternoon, Kyle realized the fuel tank was getting low. He turned to Rianna, allowing himself to study her for the first time since he'd had her in his arms. His muscles tightened at the memory, but he determinedly ignored the reaction.

Once his hormones were under control, he had gotten over the anger at her rejection. She'd prevented them from committing a major act of stupidity. Pregnancy might not be a concern, but he didn't have any condoms with him. It shook him to think he would have engaged in unprotected sex with a woman who'd shared her body with scum like Haroldson.

The thought both disgusted and infuriated him. The disgust was normal, the anger wasn't, and that worried him. He had no business getting more deeply involved.

Aside from Margie, there hadn't been many serious relationships in his life. In his early years, he'd been too focused on his career to think about long-term commitments. Since Margie, he'd been too wary. Anytime he got involved, it was with the clear understanding that he wasn't looking for permanency.

He should be thanking Rianna for calling a halt to an explosive situation, but he couldn't find the words.

She'd put on a pair of pink shorts with a white, cropped top that partially bared her midriff. Her hair looked clean, soft and shiny. Her arms and legs already looked a shade darker and just a little sunburned.

He'd been aware of her activity ever since the movie ended, but now he realized she'd been baking. The scent of cookies filled the galley, making his mouth water. He couldn't remember the last time he'd had freshly baked cookies.

"We need to refuel," he said, capturing her attention.

She looked directly at him, but her expression remained guarded.

"According to this map, there's a huge dock called Burnside at the other end of the lake. I'm heading there now."

Rianna nodded. "It might be better to steer clear of the dock where we left the car. That way none of the staff will get too familiar with the sight of us."

"We need to call Sullivan," he added, "but we can't use a local pay phone. Do you have a cellular?"

"Yes, but it's probably of no use out here. It should work once we get to a little higher elevation."

"Okay, then, we'll dock, refuel and take a hike until we can get a signal."

Rianna merely nodded, looking more subdued than he'd ever seen her. It made him feel guilty, yet irritated by the guilt. He searched for a way to ease the disturbing tension between them.

"You sharing any of those cookies? They sure smell good," he said, his tone light as he offered an olive branch.

The innocent pleasure that lit her features made a knot in his gut. She offered him a tentative smile along with the cookies, and the knot tightened, a sure sign that he was beginning to care too much. He knew better than to get emotionally involved, yet she made it hard to maintain an impersonal distance.

"They're just the packaged kind you slice and bake," she warned, easing more of the strained atmosphere.

"Beggars can't be choosers," he said, taking a handful. He thanked her and turned back to the wheel.

The refueling didn't take much time. After they'd finished, Kyle steered them into an empty birth where he secured the boat. Rianna grabbed her oversize bag and they started climbing the winding path toward the highway.

People and cars came and went, but no one paid them much attention. They were just another couple of strangers in an area swarming with vacationers. They walked steadily uphill for half an hour, and then settled onto a wooden bench while Rianna called Sullivan.

"The call's being forwarded," she said. "He's probably not home from the office yet."

Kyle leaned his head closer so that he could hear any conversation, but the move brought his face disturbingly close to hers. Close enough that he could smell the flowery scent of her shampoo. His pulse reacted, and then he heard the *click* of a connection.

"Sullivan."

"It's Phantom," said Rianna.

"You and Tremont okay?"

"We're fine," said Kyle. "How's everything on your end? Is Gregory behind bars?"

Sullivan's tone was grim. "Not yet."

"Why not?" they demanded in unison.

"The district attorney got the indictment, but we're

waiting on a search warrant for his estate. As soon as we have it, we'll arrest him. I don't want to give him an opportunity to have evidence destroyed. We want to take him and his cohorts by surprise, or they'll go into hiding behind a bunch of high-priced lawyers.''

''Sounds like a solid plan,'' said Tremont.

''Is there anything I should look for besides his business records?''

''My suite of rooms is on the northeast corner of the house,'' explained Rianna. ''The closet has a circular clothes rack with a center section portioned off for shoes. That's where you'll find the videotapes I couldn't smuggle out with me. There should be five. It's important that you keep the one labeled 'Party.' The rest can be turned in to the agency.''

''Why should I keep any of them? You know it won't be valid evidence unless it's legally confiscated during the search.''

''It's not part of the evidence,'' she insisted. ''It's personal and so important, Donald. You have to get all the tapes and keep that one for me. Don't trust another soul with it.''

''Whatever you say. I'll take care of it myself.''

''Promise?''

''On my life,'' he assured her, then added, ''We're going to get him.''

Kyle felt Rianna relax, only then realizing how tense she'd been during the conversation. His curiosity about her just went up a couple more notches. What kind of tape had she hidden? Was it personally incriminating? Maybe an x-rated video of the two of them? The thought made his gut clench.

He supposed it could be some kind of weird or deviant game Haroldson played. Maybe he'd taped her without her knowledge, or in a compromising situation. She wouldn't want it to fall into the wrong hands. The idea made him furious.

His voice held a low throb of anger as he spoke to Sullivan. "We've got to go. What next?"

"Stay low and call again tomorrow about the same time. I should have good news by then."

"Is Haroldson still proclaiming that his fiancée's been kidnapped?"

"Yeah, but I didn't have to disclose Rianna's identity. Someone tipped the press off to another possibility."

"What possibility?"

"That Haroldson's fiancée wasn't kidnapped, but ran off with her lover. A much younger man."

Kyle tilted his head enough to lock gazes with Rianna. He watched her eyes darken at the suggestion, and then she lowered her lashes to hide her reaction.

The ploy amused him, easing some of the tightness in his chest. "You wouldn't have been responsible for that bit of gossip, would you?"

Sullivan's response was all innocence. "I'm just doing my part to keep my FBI buddies in North Carolina informed. And you know how the media always jumps on every new angle."

Kyle smiled and glanced at Rianna again. She looked equally pleased by Sullivan's tactics.

"Sounds like you've got everything under control. We'll get back to you tomorrow."

Rianna said goodbye and closed the phone. Then she looked up at him. "Is there someone you'd like to call?"

He shook his head, wondering if anyone aside from Sullivan worried about her. During his years at the agency, he had found it impossible to sustain close relationships, but then, he'd always been a loner.

Except for Margie. Friends who had tolerated long absences were rare, but Margie had understood and been a true friend. He'd never forgive himself for not being there when his partner needed him most. On that last fatal assignment.

All the more reason to see that Haroldson rotted in hell.

"We'd better get back to the boat," he said.

Kyle studied their surroundings as they retraced their path to the dock. When the path narrowed, Rianna took the lead. She stepped around a rock, and he accidentally bumped into her, but they quickly severed the contact.

One touch was enough to stir his imagination. He'd fought to suppress the mental image of her on that chaise—her lush body glistening in the sunshine and clothed in nothing but a few narrow strips of cloth.

Her breasts had been plump, their peaks beading into fat buttons when he'd teased them with water. Her mouth, so eager and responsive. God, what a luscious mouth. He could have feasted on it for hours.

And her legs.

Kyle stared at her backside when she stepped ahead of him again. Her hips were slim but nicely rounded. She had long, well-toned legs. Great legs. He could still feel the strength of her thighs wrapped around him, and the heat of her body arching against his. He'd almost lost it completely.

He had never wanted a woman more, had never wanted to bury himself in someone and claim full possession. He wasn't the possessive type. Never had been. He'd never experienced such a fierce desire to conquer and possess. Not until this morning, and Rianna.

Need still clawed through him, but there's no way he'd act on it now. The timing was all wrong. She might have been as hot as he'd been, but she hadn't minced words when she'd wanted to shoot him down. Her panicked ''no'' had been as subtle as a knee to the groin.

They boarded the houseboat with no more than a passing nod to a couple of strangers. Everybody had their own agenda and nobody had the time or inclination to chat, which worked in their favor. Blending into the crowd had never been more satisfying.

''You want to take it out this time?'' he asked, after making a quick security check through the houseboat.

''Sure.''

Rianna preceded him into the cabin and took a seat behind the wheel. She started the engine while he untied the mooring ropes. Then she slowly steered them through the maze of docks and boat traffic until they were in the main waterway again.

''My turn to cook.'' He joined her in the cabin area and helped himself to another cookie. They were delicious. ''What'll it be?''

''What can you cook?''

Kyle rummaged through the refrigerator. ''How about some grilled pork chops and baked potatoes? I can handle that.''

''Perfect.''

They ate their meal a half-hour later after dropping anchor in another small cove. She complimented his cooking skills and ate everything on her plate. Both were careful not to make too much eye contact or

broach sensitive subjects. Studied politeness became
the rule of thumb.

The sky grew cloudy at dusk and a small shower
kept them inside the cabin. Kyle watched a baseball
game while Rianna curled up on the sofa with a book.
He divided his attention between the TV and her, until
the hunger in him reared its ugly head again.

By the time the rain stopped around ten o'clock, he
was more than ready to escape the confines of the
cabin. The sky had cleared, so he wanted a last look
around the area.

"I'm going up on deck for a while."

Rianna glanced up from her book. Then she closed
it and laid it aside. "I'm getting tired, but I'd like to
sit outside for a few minutes before I call it a night."

"Grab a towel for your chair. It'll be wet."

He followed her up the ladder, trying hard to ignore
the gentle sway of her behind and the legs that were
driving him crazy. As soon as they reached the deck,
he distanced himself and flopped down in one of the
lounge chairs. Rianna sat in the one she'd used earlier
in the day.

A silent groan rumbled in his chest at the sight of
her. She appealed to him even more than she had earlier. Her cautious reserve made her all the more alluring.

"Do you have a headache?" he asked.

Rianna glanced at him with a quizzical expression.
"No, why do you ask?"

"You're rubbing the back of your neck again. I've
seen you do it several times in the past few days. I
thought maybe you suffer from tension headaches."

"No, I just have a sore spot on my neck."

She hesitated, making him wonder if she intended to explain or leave him in the dark. Then she continued.

"I had a weird little accident while I was at Gregory's estate. I'm still not sure how it happened. I guess Gregory and I bumped into each other at the bottom of the stairs. I cracked the back of my head on the corner of the newel. It bled so much that it needed stitches."

"He took you to the hospital?"

Rianna laughed softly. "When you have the kind of money and clout Gregory has, they bring the hospital to you. Some doctor friend of his rushed to the house. He administered a local anesthetic, put a couple of stitches in the back of my neck, and went on his way again. I hardly felt a thing."

"You were never unconscious? You're sure Haroldson wasn't somehow responsible?"

"At first I wondered if I'd blown my cover, and he was planning to drug me or something, but he seemed genuinely concerned. He and the doctor were very solicitous."

"Don't you need to have the stitches removed?"

"He said they'd dissolve naturally."

"And the cut is still hurting?"

"It doesn't hurt, it just throbs once in a while."

"Maybe it's infected. Lake water is full of bacteria."

"It's not that sensitive. I meant to have Paulo check it when he did my hair. I forgot, but he'd have noticed if it looked red or irritated."

"I can take a look at it in the morning if you want," Kyle offered, knowing she wasn't likely to ask.

"Thanks, I'll let you know if it starts to bother me again."

He doubted that, but let the subject drop. Looking

at her and thinking about her was distracting enough. So much so that he forced himself to focus on their surroundings.

The inky sky was brilliant with its canopy of stars. Water lapped lazily against the shore, the waves rocking them in their wake. Breathing deeply, he let the warm, rain-washed freshness of the air seep into his senses.

It soothed, while arousing, creating a sensual delight and bringing his body to full, aching awareness. The kind of awareness that no amount of moonlight would soothe. He wondered if she felt it as strongly as he did.

The night was meant for loving, for oh-so-slow caresses, hot, tangled bodies, and deep, drugging kisses. But making love wasn't on their agenda. The woman he lusted after didn't want involvement, and had ruthlessly reminded him of that.

It might be a very long night.

Chapter 6

The next morning dawned clear and bright. Rianna heard Kyle moving around the galley as soon as the sun had peaked over the horizon. She'd slept fitfully and knew he'd been restless, too. It didn't help to be sleeping within a few feet, wanting each other so desperately, yet knowing they dared not succumb to the attraction.

The smell of coffee drew her from her bed, just as it had the previous morning. This time, she carefully entered the galley area, making sure she didn't collide with his hard, male body. Still, he pinned her with a probing gaze that made her heart stutter. She offered a tentative smile, and he offered a caffeine fix. By mutual agreement, they carried it to the upper deck.

After a few minutes to appreciate another new day, Kyle decided he wanted grilled fish for breakfast.

"I hate to sound negative," she reminded, hiding her

grin, "but so far, the fish seem to have eluded capture."

He flashed her a very male frown before his eyes lit with challenge. "Maybe you think you can do better?"

Rianna chuckled, shaking her head. "I know my limitations, and I know absolutely nothing about catching fish."

"Any reasonable, intelligent person can learn," he taunted.

Never one to resist a challenge, she took him up on it. Then he hauled out the fishing gear and began coaching her in the basics of freshwater fishing.

The lesson involved a lot of detailed instruction, concentrated effort and good-natured banter. The attraction between them heightened with each touch of a hand, brush of a shoulder or shared laugh, yet they didn't allow it to sabotage their pleasure.

"The fish aren't cooperating very well, and I'm starved," she said after an hour without success. "How about I fix some breakfast, and we put fish on the lunch menu?"

He sighed and shook his head in disgust, then offered her a rare grin. It stole her breath. His eyes were as blue as the morning sky, his expression softer than she'd ever seen it, and her stomach did a crazy little flip-flop.

Hunger. It had to be hunger, she argued to herself. A man's eyes and smile couldn't really make a woman's stomach do somersaults. That only happened in the fictional world, never in real life. She'd just gone too long without food.

Her voice sounded rusty when she spoke. "How about milk, cookies and a banana or two to hold us until we catch some unsuspecting little fishes?"

"Okay by me."

She quickly made her exit and collected some food from the galley, all the while breathing deeply and lecturing herself on the idiocy of their attraction. When she returned on deck, she was calmer and managed to ignore the tension while they shared a snack.

Shortly after they'd eaten, the fish started biting. Rianna caught two nice-size bass, and couldn't believe how much she enjoyed the small success. She caught a third one, then turned the pole over to Kyle, who caught a couple more.

Once they had enough for a meal, they decided to call it quits. The traffic on the lake had increased, and they'd been on deck long enough. She went to the galley to get a pan of water while Kyle cleaned the fish.

When she returned, he surprised her by scooping her into his arms. "Hold your breath," he commanded.

Not again, she thought. Sensing his tension, she didn't bother to argue, just wrapped her arms around his neck and clung. Then they were whizzing down the slide. This time she gulped some air and prepared herself for the chilly depths. Instead of trying to fight her way free of Kyle's grasp, she clung to him and they surfaced together.

The first thing she did after catching her breath was pound on his chest. "What the hell was that for?"

"Helicopter," he warned as he urged her toward the shadows at the back of the boat.

They each grabbed a rung of the swim ladder and ducked out of sight. Arms and legs tangled, then they went as still as possible, making no visible waves. They watched, barely breathing, as a helicopter slowly made its way along the main body of the lake, from east to west.

"It has some sort of logo on it," she whispered.

"It could be a television news crew. Or some kind of law enforcement 'copter."

The helicopter flew over the center of the lake without veering from its straightforward path or coming too near their cove. It didn't hover long in any one spot.

Kyle had her sandwiched between the boat and his big body. Rianna couldn't move, so she finally slid her free arm around his waist and let him tread water for both of them. A shiver raced over her as her palm slid over his hard, flat stomach, but it had nothing to do with fear. She pressed herself closer, peering over his shoulder and putting her mouth near his ear.

"You don't think we could be seen or attacked from the air, do you?" She found it hard to believe that anyone could have tracked their escape. They'd been so careful.

"Tracked maybe, but not attacked. Haroldson's men wouldn't be that stupid, but they could be searching by air."

"That logo looks more like a resort emblem. The owners probably police the area, don't they? Or maybe they're doing some promotional tours."

"It wouldn't take much for Haroldson to finagle a free ride for his goons. He's a wealthy man and could pretend to have an interest in the resort operation."

"They probably take prospective clients out for joy rides," she said, absently wondering how his body could be so warm in the chill of the water. Everywhere they touched, she felt the heat of him. "I'll bet this place is impressive from the air."

He nodded, and they watched the helicopter depart, knowing they shouldn't move out of hiding until it could no longer be seen or heard.

As the drone of the engine faded, she became even more aware of how their bodies were entwined. The hair on his thighs tickled hers, sending little shivers of reaction over her skin. Her breasts, stomach and thighs were tightly pressed against his broad back and tight rear, stimulating every tiny nerve.

Excitement sung through her veins. This sexy renegade stirred her senses as no other man had ever done. It wouldn't do to let him know how easily he could throw her hormones into a tizzy. She tried to ease some space between them so that he wouldn't feel how tightly her nipples had hardened.

"I think it's safe now," he said, pulling free of her grasp and shoving himself clear of the boat.

Missing the feel of him the instant he moved, Rianna took a slow, deep breath. After regaining some control, she hauled herself up the ladder on legs that quivered. Kyle threatened her hard-won independence. She was beginning to care too much. So much so that his smile and his touch made her ache with longing. And he'd slipped past her emotional guard—that worried her even more.

She showered while he finished cleaning the fish, then he took his turn in the shower. Subdued, and lost in their own thoughts, they grilled their fish and shared a quiet lunch.

Shortly afterward, they pulled up anchor and headed back toward the cove where he'd found the jogging trail the previous day. Rianna contented herself with watching the speedboats, tubers and Jet Skiers who zipped by them, but she didn't venture on deck.

By mid-afternoon, they'd dropped anchor again, and Kyle announced that he wanted to take another run. He warned her to keep her gun within reach and to listen for a return of the helicopter. They repeated the transfer of his shoes, socks and gun. She watched until he'd swum to shore, strapped the gun to his ankle and donned his socks and shoes. Then he climbed the boulders that lined the bank.

Once he'd disappeared from view, she changed into her lime-green bikini and pulled a white T-shirt over it. She'd swim and work on her tan when Kyle returned, but in the meantime, planned to finish her book while she waited.

As interesting as she found the story, she quickly grew too restless to concentrate. An instinctive edginess propelled her toward the back of the boat. It was hard to stay cooped up inside when the sunshine and water beckoned, but she knew that wasn't the real problem. The scare this morning had her senses on high alert. She decided to watch the water traffic from the back of the boat until her partner returned.

Moving to the windowed back door, she watched one speedboat cruise by pulling two skiers. It looked like so much fun that she promised herself to try it someday. Another boat passed pulling an inflated rubber tube with two teenagers clinging to the sides and bouncing wildly. That looked like a rough ride. Laughing softly, she decided she'd have to think twice about trying that.

Two jet skiers, driving dangerously fast, went zipping by next, then a pontoon and a slow-moving houseboat. The decks were crowded with people of all ages whose laughter drifted across the water. Rianna felt a pang of envy as she remembered her own family's carefree vacation.

What would it be like to live a normal, happy life without the constant fear of discovery? Without the need to run and hide like a criminal, always fearful? She'd given up much hope of ever knowing that particular contentment.

Love and marriage had never been part of her long-term goals. Those goals hadn't stretched beyond bringing a murderer to justice. She wanted Gregory to pay for the death of her parents and brother. Although she loved children, she'd always feared her biological clock would run out long before she could consider a normal relationship.

As the next speedboat passed, her lungs constricted on a harsh gasp, then her pulse lurched into overdrive. The boat held four big men and not one of them had the look of a vacationer. The silhouette of one in particular looked too much like Rudy to be a coincidence.

Rianna's survival instincts kicked in, her only thought, *escape*. There was no time to gather belongings other than her gun. She checked the safety and tucked it into her bikini bottoms as she raced through the boat. The last thing she heard before diving off the front deck was the sound of the speedboat throttling to turn and head back her way.

She dove deep and swam underwater, kicking and pulling with all her might. Knowing she wouldn't have time to reach the shore and climb the bank where Kyle had gone, she headed for the outcropping of land that separated one cove from the next. If she could get around it before she was spotted, she'd have a chance.

A few minutes later, she surfaced to catch her breath and get her bearings. With the houseboat between her and the intruders, she couldn't tell how close they'd gotten, so she dove again and swam until her lungs burned and threatened to explode. The third time she

surfaced, she found herself at the edge of the neighboring cove.

With one final sprint, she rounded the bend of land
and put the outcropping of solid rock between her and
the speedboat. Confident they couldn't see her now, she
surfaced and began to swim across the wide stretch of
water.

The sound of men shouting gave her the extra
strength to drag herself ashore. Her chest heaved and
her limbs trembled from exertion. Her pulse roared in
her ears. Catching some much-needed air, she squeezed
excess water from her hair and shirt, frantically searching the bank for a place to climb.

She cursed herself for not remembering shoes, then
stumbled across the beach and started up the slippery
ascent. Years of strenuous workouts paid off as every
muscle in her body strained to the max. Clawing and
dragging herself up the rocky bank, she reached the top
in a burst of adrenaline, and then lunged between two
giant boulders.

For the next few minutes, she lay sprawled, face-
down where she'd fallen. The semiautomatic poked her
in the stomach, still secure, yet unreliable now that it
had been immersed in water. Her breathing was harsh,
but she smothered the sound in the tall, thick grass
while struggling to regain some strength.

Kyle.

She was going to kill him. Maybe with her bare
hands. Her fists clenched at the thought. Various methods of punishment and torture drifted through her mind,
gradually replacing the terror she'd just experienced.

How could he have betrayed her?

There was no other explanation for the timely arrival
of Gregory's men; no possible way they could have

tracked her down. Grinding her teeth in frustration, she wondered if she'd been a fool to trust him.

Her heart felt cold and heavy, clutched in a viselike pain, he'd been the rare exception to her longtime rule of not letting anyone get too close. She'd started to care for him.

Had it all been an elaborate scheme? His disgust for Gregory, his concern for her safety, and all the cautions he'd suggested? She didn't want to think she could be so wrong about someone, but she intended to find out for sure.

Lifting her head, she searched the immediate area for the jogging path he'd described. At least that part of his story was true. She saw a path and let her gaze travel to where it disappeared into a line of trees. Her pulse had begun to quiet, but it went berserk again when she caught sight of him about a hundred yards distant.

He ran at a slow, steady pace, his arms and legs moving with an economy of motion. His body glistened with sweat, and his chest heaved gently. Rianna's pulse skipped another few beats. He looked so normal, so sexy and so damn unconcerned.

She frowned. Could he be that good an actor? If he'd brought them here, why hadn't he just disappeared? He looked so natural, as though he'd been enjoying a carefree run. Why hadn't he just kept running toward the marina? Did he plan to help them trap her, or continue his vacation after she'd been hauled away?

Or could he be as much a victim as she?

Rising slowly to her feet, she reached under her T-shirt and locked her hand around the gun. It might not work, but neither of them could be sure of that. At least for now, she had the upper hand.

Kyle had covered most of the distance between them before she stepped clear of the boulder and into his line of view. He stopped immediately, his features tightening in concern. His gaze dropped to the gun and then back to her strained expression.

"What the hell?"

"You tell me," said Rianna as she leveled the Glock at his midsection and flipped the safety off. She braced her right hand with her left, and her attention never wavered from his face. She desperately wanted to believe his confusion was genuine, but her life depended on caution. She couldn't let her heart rule reason.

"Why'd you leave the boat?" he asked, panting as he tried to catch his breath. "What's going on?"

"We've got company."

Kyle's gaze swiftly flew toward the embankment, searching for the intruders. After aiming a blank glance at her, he headed to the bank above the cove where they'd left the boat. He turned his back to her without hesitation, as though she didn't present any real threat. Or, like her, he realized she couldn't afford to fire and alert anyone to her whereabouts.

Rianna gritted her teeth, clutched the gun and called herself a fool, but went with her instincts. If Kyle had any knowledge of the ambush, he deserved an Oscar. He looked genuinely surprised and worried.

Moving from boulder to boulder along the bank, he stayed hidden and waved her to stay back. She ignored the unspoken order and followed until they were directly above the cove where they'd anchored. From their vantage point, they could see the houseboat without being visible from the water.

The speedboat had pulled alongside their boat. Two men stayed on the smaller craft while two others searched the houseboat. Rianna recognized Rudy and another of Gregory's employees, by the name of Tabone.

"Nowhere in sight, but they were here." Rudy's voice carried to them. "Search everything, Tabone."

They watched as he moved onto the front deck and did a visual search of the cove. Then he pulled something out of his pocket and waved it in front of him. At first, Rianna thought it might be a gun, but then she thought it looked more like a cell phone. She just couldn't figure why he'd be waving it around.

Kyle touched her arm, urging her to back away from the rock barriers. It wasn't likely that anyone could see them, but they cautiously retraced their steps until they'd returned to the jogging path.

"What did he have?" she finally whispered. Still not sure he could be trusted, she kept the gun leveled at his midsection.

He studied the gun and then her features, his jaw tight and expression grim. "Use it or put it away," he demanded tersely.

Tension quivered between them until she slowly flipped the safety on the gun and tucked it back into her swimsuit.

He grabbed her arm and started pulling her along the path to a clump of trees. "He's got some kind of electronic tracking device."

It made sense, but it didn't make sense. "That would work if he had a signal to follow, but there's no way. How the hell did they find us? Even if they traced our call to Donald, that wouldn't have given our exact location. This place is huge!"

"They have to be honing in on a direct signal."

"That's not possible. I checked everything I brought

out of the estate. Nobody knew where the car was garaged, so they couldn't have bugged it,'' she insisted, thinking aloud. ''I mailed all the jewelry to Maine. Everything else I brought with me is on the boat, so they'd have found the bug when they boarded. It doesn't fit.''

Kyle's expression grew grimmer, his eyes going cold and hard while his jaws clenched. ''Unless it's on you,'' he said.

She didn't like the way he was looking at her, and liked his suggestion even less. ''Where?'' she demanded in a frustrated whisper. ''I'm barely dressed, and I know there's no bug in my gun. I'm not wearing any jewelry, and I haven't even had a cavity filled since I met Gregory.''

''What if it's implanted under your skin?'' he suggested, studying her intently.

Rianna froze, eyes widening in horror. A terrible chill raced over her, freezing, and then numbing her with shock. Her lungs constricted painfully, her throat growing so tight that she could barely whisper the next questions.

''How? Where?''

He pulled her close and spun her around. Then he lifted the hair off the back of her neck and looked at her nape. His voice held a feral snarl when he finally spoke.

''What if your weird accident wasn't an accident at all? What if Haroldson had a device implanted in your neck? It wouldn't have to be very big,'' he added, running a finger lightly over the stitches.

Rianna's stomach roiled. It made sense, and it explained the strange accident. She slapped a hand over her mouth to keep from screaming in outrage and denial. Her body became one giant tremor, shaking her to the very core.

"It's possible," she whispered gruffly. "It sounds like something he'd do. He's fanatic about his possessions and that's what he considered me. He has no morals and no conscience."

Kyle muttered a string of vicious obscenities, and then jerked her around to face him. He gave her a fierce hug that helped soften some of her shock, but it was way too brief. A tracking devise was beyond her worst nightmare, and she was badly shaken.

"We've got to get away from here." His warm breath touched her ear. "Right now, we're shielded by those boulders. The signal probably can't penetrate them, but as soon as they come over that embankment, they'll be able to pinpoint our location."

"What can we do?" she asked, knowing what a wild animal must feel like to be pinned in the headlights of a car.

Kyle was already reaching for the gun at his ankle. He unfastened the strap and then whipped it around her neck, positioning the gun over the scar on her nape.

"We run for it. Hopefully, the metal of the gun will interfere with the signal until we come up with a better solution."

As soon as he'd secured the holster around her neck, he turned to lead the way. Rianna relegated the sick terror of a body invasion to the back of her mind. She couldn't allow herself to dwell on this latest atrocity. Survival came first.

They'd only gone a short distance before she realized an additional handicap. "I'm barefoot," she called softly to Kyle.

He stopped abruptly, turned and stared down at her

bare feet. "You can't run this path like that. There're too many sticks and rocks. You'll have to ride piggyback."

She stared at him as though he'd lost his mind. He'd already been jogging for an hour. She was way too heavy to carry, and reluctant to be totally dependent on him. Remembering the last time she'd wrapped her legs around him, she panicked briefly, then latched on to the first lame excuse that leapt to mind.

"You smell like dirty socks."

He looked stunned by the inanity of her comment. Then his eyes softened in understanding. "You smell like dead fish," he countered gently. "Now, get on."

She grimaced and conceded, knowing they were wasting precious time. He turned and leaned down so she could hop onto his back. Then he hefted her up until he had a firm grip on her thighs. She wrapped her arms around his upper chest, trying not to strangle him.

He ran deeper into the woods and splashed through a shallow stream of water, then followed it long enough to throw off anyone who tried to track them on foot. After they'd traveled a mile or so, he moved back toward the regular path, then stayed parallel with it without actually using it.

Rianna ducked her head to avoid low-hanging branches for a while, and then buried her face against his neck. He smelled of sweat and man. The heat of him scorched her inner thighs, belly and chest, making her extremely aware of every hard, muscled inch of his body. His pulse became hers as it pounded rapidly through his veins. It was an experience unlike anything she'd ever known.

"How far do you plan to run?" she whispered in his ear.

"Another few miles."

"You can't carry me that far!"

Kyle slowed, and then stopped just before a clearing with several cabins. He let Rianna slide to the ground. She sat still, watching him closely while he struggled to catch his breath.

"We have two choices," he finally said. "We can try to make it to the marina and hot-wire the car, or we can hide out for a while in one of the deserted cabins around here."

"There's a key to the car hidden under the right front bumper, but we can't risk going after it," she said.

"Why?"

"If Rudy searched the houseboat, he found the marina rental receipt. It has the car's license number. He'll go there next and either have it watched or plant something worse than a bug."

Kyle swore, raking a hand through his hair in frustration. "We can't hitch a ride while that gun's strapped to your neck, so we'll have to hide. I've seen a couple of cabins that don't look inhabited right now."

"You can leave me and hitch a ride to town to find some transportation."

"No!" His response was harsh. He glared at her. "We stay together. Rudy and his men will have to split up if they search the whole area. As long as we're together, one man at a time isn't a threat. We'll go to a cabin and formulate a new plan."

Rianna didn't argue. She didn't want to part ways with him, yet she wondered at his motives. Did he have his own agenda for keeping her safe? Some unknown reason for not wanting her out of his sight? The answers weren't forthcoming, so she nudged the questions to the back of her mind. She'd worked solo for too long and didn't want to go it alone anymore.

"The path goes behind that group of cabins. I didn't see anyone around earlier, but we should try to walk past like we're taking a stroll. Since you're barefoot, we'll go slow."

She nodded and fell into step beside him until they'd covered the short distance across the clearing. Once they were out of sight of the rental cabins, Kyle leaned down and hefted her onto his back once more.

"You're going to owe me a serious rubdown," he insisted, picking up his pace again.

Rianna smiled against his neck, and unconsciously tightened her grip on him. She'd reserve judgment about what she owed him. She still hadn't decided whether it would be a debt of gratitude or slow torture. Come to think of it, a full-body massage might fit the bill in either case.

Kyle left the path and veered deeper into the woods, plunging them from dappled sunlight into near darkness. He slowed down to a walk as they encountered heavier vegetation.

"Are you sure there's a cabin up here? How'd you find this place?"

"I've seen several isolated cabins, and figure they're privately owned. I followed a doe and fawn through the woods here," he explained. "They led me to the cabin with a salt-lick in the yard. Looks deserted."

He breathed deeply from exertion, and she felt every intake of breath like her own. His muscles flexed and her nerves jangled. Never having experienced such an intense physical connection, the feel of it defied description.

The small log cabin stood buried in a cluster of tall evergreens. Covered in ivy, the whole structure was nearly hidden from view. He jogged around the right side to a small back porch, and then stopped to let her slide off his back.

"You're sure nobody's living here?"

"It doesn't look like anyone's been here for a while. Maybe someone only uses it a couple of weeks a year."

"Let's just hope this isn't their week."

"Yeah," Kyle agreed. He searched the door and a small window frame for a spare key, but couldn't find one. "I hate to break in if we don't have to."

She helped to search, overturning rocks and looking under a loose wooden plank in the porch. Kyle reached above them and felt along the rafters of the roof, while she looked in and under a collection of flowerpots.

"Look!" she exclaimed.

Chapter 7

Rianna held up a key she had found under a dried fern in a clay pot. Kyle took it and ordered her to stay put while he checked the house. She reached for her gun and followed him through the narrow door. It didn't take long to establish that the cabin didn't hold any surprises. There were only two sections, a living room with a small kitchenette and a small bedroom with an even smaller bathroom.

Except for some dust and a cobweb or two, the inside of the cabin appeared neat and well cared for. The furnishings were serviceable rather than fashionable, but with homey touches like dried flower arrangements. A stone fireplace took up one entire end of the living room area.

"Not bad," said Kyle, after checking the kitchen cupboards. "It's stocked with nonperishables."

Rianna headed to the bedroom. "I hope the owners left some clothes here." She opened the closet and found a collection of outerwear that wasn't of much use, but the canvas tennis shoes thrilled her. Her feet hurt.

The dresser drawers offered a change of clothing. "Looks like this place belongs to a married couple. There's a mix of clothing," she told him as he followed her into the room.

"What sizes?"

"Large men's and medium women's. We should be okay. I think our absent host and hostess might be a little heavier than we are, but not so much that we can't borrow a few things."

"It might not hurt to add a little padding around our waists. Any disguise will help."

She agreed. The elastic on the sweatpants would stretch for extra cushioning.

"I think we should shower, eat and head out again," she said. "If we can get a ride to town, we can pick up money at the post office, pay for some transportation, and be miles from here before Rudy spreads out his search."

"You don't think it would be safer to hole up here overnight and head to town tomorrow?"

Rianna thought about spending another night like the last, trying to sleep, yet too achingly aware of her roommate. It wouldn't be wise to invite more intimacy. Besides, neither of them would rest knowing Rudy might find them at any minute.

Then there was the electronic bug buried under her skin. Her teeth clenched in anger at the thought. She wanted it out as soon as possible.

"It'll be a risk to leave, but more of a risk to stay. If you found this cabin, there's a chance Gregory's men will, too. I'd rather take our chances in town. We can appeal to the local sheriff, if necessary."

"Okay. I'll get the generator running and then get that gun off your neck."

Rianna touched her nape. The gun felt cold and heavy against her tender skin. "What can we do?"

"If I cut off the bulk of the holster, the gun can be replaced with a butter knife. It won't be pretty, but it shouldn't attract attention."

"Chokers are all the rage," she muttered grimly, "but I don't know about knife blades." Then another idea had her heading back to the kitchen area.

"We'll have to leave a big tip for our hosts." She snatched a little notepad from the refrigerator. "This is magnetic. A magnet would really scramble the signal, wouldn't it?"

"Good idea," agreed Kyle as he followed her. "We should try to pay for what we take, but all my cash is on the boat. How about you?"

His gaze slid down her body to the juncture of her thighs, making her pulse leap and her flesh tingle. She shifted her legs and responded gruffly.

"Always. I told you I never travel without cash."

"How much?"

Kyle's voice had dropped an octave. His gaze returned to her face. They stared at each other for a few tense minutes, and then made a concerted effort to shake off the sensual tension caused by his intimate perusal.

"A few hundred. Enough for a couple of days' food and lodging."

"So we don't need what you mailed to yourself in Somerset?" he asked.

"It all depends on how long we have to keep running. My stash won't stretch for transportation."

"How much did you leave in Somerset?"

"Several thousand, plus another phony ID."

He sighed. "Okay, I guess we go there next."

Dusk had fallen by the time they'd showered, changed into the borrowed clothing and eaten a cold, canned meal. Rianna had rinsed the lake water from her bikini, but wore the swimsuit under the sweats. She didn't want to be without her special storage pouch, and her hostess's bras were too big.

She'd kept her back to the brick fireplace while Kyle redesigned her leather necklace. It was far from attractive, yet not awful enough to draw unwanted attention. By the time they left the cabin, they looked like an average married couple in slightly creased casual wear and running shoes.

The trek through the woods was slow going—progress was made a few cautious yards at a time. Once they reached the main road, they hailed a teenager in a battered pickup truck. He worked at the marina, but his shift had ended, so he happily accepted twenty dollars to drive them to Somerset.

Rianna spent the ride squeezed between the two of them. The truck's gearshift was on the floor, so she had to lean against Kyle to avoid bumping it with her leg. He slid an arm across the back of the seat to give her room, but that made her feel more trapped. Every curve in the winding road had her pressing into him, and the feel of his hard body kept hers singing with excitement.

They reached the southern edge of town shortly before eleven. Kyle helped her from the truck, but she quickly withdrew her hand from his grasp. They thanked their new friend and bade him farewell, then Kyle reached for her again.

"We'd better keep our hands free for weapons," she insisted, pulling from his grip.

A lift of his brow questioned her response and the evasive action. They'd swapped guns, wrapped them in towels and secured them around their waists. The sweats didn't have pockets, but the belly pouches gave them a place to hide the weapons while adding a few inches to their waistlines. Kyle didn't argue, he just placed his left hand to the back of her waist and guided her into the shadows.

"I've heard of rolling up the sidewalks at dark, but I think this town really does it," said Rianna.

"It's a work night for most people," he added, leading her toward the post office. The occasional streetlight helped illuminate their path, yet left enough shadowy corners to make them wary.

"We'd better not go into the post office together," she said as they drew closer to their destination.

Kyle agreed. "I'll circle around back and come up the alley on the other side."

Rianna watched him disappear, her stomach sinking in an indescribable fashion. She shook her head in amazement. When and how had she let herself get so attached to the man? It was stupid to feel bereft without him by her side.

Surveying the street, she didn't notice anything out of the ordinary, so she made her way to the end of the block. The post office lobby was empty. She collected her package, and then returned the key through the drop slot. Tucking the envelope into her makeshift belly pack, she headed outside again.

After another quick glance up and down the street,

she turned toward the shadowed alley. Suddenly, all the fine hairs on her arms and neck started tingling. Rianna tensed, deciding someone aside from Kyle was causing her alarm.

She didn't react fast enough. A giant arm slammed her body against an equally solid chest. She felt the barrel of a gun pressing against her neck and immediately recognized her captor's voice.

"Well, well, sweet Samantha. Nice to see you again."

Rianna's heart rammed against her ribs, and sweat dampened her skin. She went perfectly still, barely able to breathe as Rudy's arm tightened around her arms and chest. He held her in a bruising grip—evidence that he was furious with her. She'd made a fool of him, and men in his position didn't take that lightly.

Despite his size, he moved with the speed and agility of a martial arts expert. She'd seen him work out in the gym, and knew he wouldn't be easily overpowered or outmaneuvered.

"Where's lover boy, Tony?"

He slowly nudged her forward, and she saw a dark vehicle parked a few yards down the alley.

"We decided to split up."

"Mr. Haroldson will be sorry to hear that. He was hopin' to have you both back home real soon."

An involuntary shiver raced through her at the thought. Rudy must have felt it, and he gave a bark of laughter. "You got that right, honey. You best be shakin' in your shoes. Mr. Haroldson's real upset."

Rianna briefly wondered if Gregory had been arrested. It should have happened today, but they'd had no way to call and check. It didn't seem likely, with Rudy still on the loose.

What could possibly have gone wrong? As far as she knew, Rudy was to be arrested along with several other members of Gregory's staff.

They reached the car, a small Jeep, and he shoved her against the back door on the passenger side. He pressed himself against her in a deliberate attempt to humiliate. His laughter had a lewd edge as he breathed heavily in her ear.

"I sure hope the boss lets me have a go at you, little slut," he said, thrusting his hips against her and grinding them in a disgusting attempt to demean her. "I always thought it was a waste to keep you in that big house with nobody gettin' any of this sweet body."

Another shudder of revulsion coursed through her. The touch of his body sickened her, but she forced herself not to panic. Rudy would never disobey orders, and she was relatively sure Gregory hadn't given him permission to manhandle her.

At least, not yet.

Where the hell was Kyle? Would he be coming to her rescue? He could be trusted, she sincerely believed that, but she wasn't used to depending on anyone. What if he'd been jumped by another of Gregory's men?

"Open the door," Rudy ordered.

He eased his grip on her enough to allow her to reach the handle. Then she heard the unmistakable sound of metal connecting with bone. Rudy grunted, his grip went slack, and she felt him falling to the ground.

"You okay?" asked Kyle.

She was trembling from head to foot, and leaned against the car for support. In the next instant, Kyle's arms were pulling her close. Rianna didn't resist the offer of comfort. She slid her hands around his waist and clung, feeling relieved, yet guilty for having doubted him again.

"Did he hurt you?" His tone sounded low and gruff in her ear.

She shivered again, but with a whole different emotion. Relief surged through her, accompanied by a needy, hopeful feeling that alarmed her. She eased from his grip.

"I'm okay," she insisted, shaking off the momentary weakness. "It sounded like you cracked his skull."

"Not that hard head. He'll be awake and fighting mad in a few minutes. Let's get him tied up."

"With what?"

"Check the car."

While Rianna searched the car, Kyle searched Rudy's pockets. He found the car keys, a cell phone and the electronic tracking device Rudy had used to locate her.

"Nothing in the car."

"He's wearing high-top boots. We'll use his bootlaces."

They each grabbed a foot and began unlacing Rudy's boots. Then they rolled him onto his stomach, tied his hands behind his back and secured his feet. Rudy groaned, prompting Kyle to check his head and his breathing.

"He's not bleeding. He has a goose egg, and his breathing is fine. He'll live."

"What now? Leave him here? Take him to the police? The emergency room?"

"Help me roll him to the side of the alley so he won't get run over," he said. They half lifted, half dragged the big man off the concrete. "We'll leave him and put some distance between us before we call the authorities. Then they can deal with him.''

"Maybe there's a warrant out for his arrest," added Rianna. "If Gregory's been arrested, there should be warrants out for Rudy and Tabone, too."

They moved back to the car. Kyle automatically headed for the driver's side, so Rianna climbed into the passenger seat.

"Think it's safe to take his car? It could be bugged," she said.

"It's got rental tags," he reassured her as the engine roared to life. "They wouldn't have had a reason to bug it."

"Probably not." She pulled her seat belt into place. "But Tabone and the others can recognize it, so we'll have to find something else."

"Later," he insisted. "First thing we have to do is find a hospital and get that metal out of your neck. I've got Rudy's tracking device, but there could be others."

"There's a regional hospital near here. As anxious as I am to have this thing removed, I'd feel more comfortable if we headed north a while before we stop."

Kyle glanced toward her, then back to the road. "You're sure?"

"I'm sure I don't want any more confrontations tonight."

The brief brush with Rudy had made her physically ill. She'd never expected such a violent physical and emotional reaction. It still had her shaken, and that scared her senseless.

How could she bear to go back and face them? Even for a trial? She loathed everything and everybody associated with Gregory Haroldson. The loathing had deepened over the past few months. It wasn't until she'd been free of it that she'd realized how profoundly the assignment had traumatized her.

"Lexington's a couple of hours north," said Kyle, glancing at her again. "You sure you're okay?"

She sensed his concern, but couldn't begin to explain her emotional turmoil. Hugging herself to ward off the deep-seated chill, she answered in what she hoped was a convincing tone.

"I'm fine."

"You cold?"

"A little."

He turned on the heat even though the temperature in the Jeep was plenty warm. The small, sensitive action made Rianna feel weepy and confused. She blinked back tears and stared out the windshield as they left the lights of town behind them.

Darkness settled around them as they hit the open highway. Her thoughts churned along with the echo of tires on the road. Memories of the months spent in Gregory's home kept whirring through her mind like a movie reel, making her more and more agitated.

She'd taken on a phony identity for a noble cause. But no matter how she tried to rationalize her actions, she still felt cheapened by all the pretense and deceit. She'd become someone she neither knew nor liked. Somewhere along the path to justice, she'd lost herself, and it scared the hell out of her.

Despite the warmth of the car, she could quell neither the chills coursing through her nor the sick rolling in her stomach. Each passing mile brought a more frantic need to run and hide. Not just from Gregory, but from life and all the emotional upheaval that went with it.

She'd known going into the assignment that the risks amounted to a lot more than physical danger. She'd been repeatedly lectured by Donald and warned by the psychologists. She'd read all the data and known what to expect.

So why didn't any of it comfort her now? Why were her hands as cold as ice? Why couldn't she steady the shaky, queasy feeling of shock?

They'd been traveling for less than an hour when Kyle slowed the car, pulled to the side of the road and shut off the engine. The unexpected action jarred Rianna out of her silent misery. She glanced around them, seeing nothing but shadows beyond the highway, and then she turned to stare at Kyle.

He took a deep breath, his chest expanding and then relaxing. Next he unclipped his seat belt and hers, reaching to gather her into his arms. The instant she realized he was offering comfort, she launched herself at him. Wrapping her arms tightly around his neck, she clung to him as though her next breath depended on the contact.

His arms tightened in response. He pulled her across his lap as she pressed closer, burying her face in the curve of his shoulder. He felt hard and wonderfully solid, his sweatshirt damp from the excessive heat in the car. He'd sacrificed his comfort to try to soothe her, and that made her feel even more pathetic.

He hugged her tightly, his warmth permeating deep into her bones, chasing away the coldness. A sob clawed at her throat, and a tremor shook her as she battled her personal demons.

"I'm sorry," he said roughly, rubbing his face against her hair. "I should have gotten to you sooner.

I wanted to make sure none of the others were near, but I shouldn't have let Rudy touch you.''

She shook her head in denial. ''It's not just Rudy,'' she said, although his repulsive treatment had triggered her reactions. ''It's the whole dirty business.''

''Yeah, I know.''

His low, soothing tone seeped into her ear and her heart. She realized that he really did understand.

''It's okay,'' he added, pressing a kiss to her temple. ''You're just crashing a little. Don't be scared.''

Rianna knew he'd experienced similar situations. Still, she tried to explain. ''For a little while, on the boat,'' she whispered roughly, ''I felt so clean and normal.''

''I know.''

Suddenly, she needed to let it all out, to get the terrible secrets off her mind. ''I loved the power and adrenaline of living the lie, but I hate myself for feeling anything but disgust. I want Gregory punished, yet I wonder if I'm any better than him with all the lies and deceit.''

''There's no doubt about that,'' he assured, gently stroking her back. ''Bringing him down means avenging a lot of people and saving a lot more.''

''I know. I keep telling myself that, over and over again,'' she whispered. ''I know what I did was important, personally and professionally. It just makes me sick. All of it. The games, the deception, the running and hiding. I just want it to be done.''

Kyle nuzzled her neck, still speaking quietly and calmly in her ear. ''The psychologists warned you, didn't they?''

She nodded, rubbing her head against his, soothed

by the contact. "I know all the psychological explanations. It's just harder to deal with the reality of it."

"Yeah," he gruffly agreed. "It's harder. Especially as deep as you infiltrated."

Rianna felt the increased tension in his body and hugged him even harder. She stopped wallowing in self-pity long enough to wonder what he felt and thought about her assignment. She'd let him believe she'd slept with a murderer and thief.

A heavy dose of guilt assailed her. Kyle had done nothing but help and protect her, yet she'd constantly doubted him and his motives. She'd deceived him by letting him believe a lie, and she'd used that lie to protect her own cowardly fear of involvement. It was past time to level with him, and risk a deeper involvement.

"I was inside the operation, but not as deep as you think," she confessed in a small voice. "Gregory and I were never lovers."

Kyle stiffened, and then eased her away until they could see each other. Moonlight bathed his taut features.

"Explain."

Rianna flattened her hands on his chest and dropped her gaze from the intensity of his. "Gregory's main interest in me was social status. I made it clear from the beginning that I wouldn't have sex until after we were married. He agreed, and kept his end of the bargain."

"He just wanted a pretense of normalcy?"

"Yes."

She dared a glance at him, but he looked even more fierce.

"So you didn't actually prostitute yourself for the

assignment?'' he growled, lifting her off his lap and putting some space between them.

His words stung, and her breathing stilled. Her next words were hard to get past the dryness in her throat. ''That's what you think of me? That I'm some kind of whore who'd use my body to gather evidence?''

''You tell me what to think.''

Rianna felt a small surge of anger, but it was quickly squelched. Sadness and regret followed. As much as she wanted his unconditional respect, she couldn't blame him for thinking the worst. She'd encouraged everyone to believe it.

''Gregory and I had a pact. He wanted a society wife, and I pretended to be penniless. That gained me entrance to his estate.''

Kyle's gaze never wavered. He stared at her with unblinking intensity. ''You're saying you never slept with him?''

''Never.'' The thought nauseated her. ''He has a mistress. She's just not suitable wife material.''

''Damn!''

His curse echoed loud and long as he continued to glare at her. She could almost feel him struggling with the truth. A myriad of expressions crossed his features—first shock and disbelief, then relief, and then renewed anger.

''We've been living in each other's pockets for the past few days, and you knew it bugged the hell out of me,'' he growled. ''Why didn't you tell me the truth?''

She was silent for a minute as she studied his tense expression. Then she warily made another confession. ''I didn't know if I could trust you.''

He rubbed his jaw and stared out the windshield. Rianna held her breath, wondering if she'd completely alienated him with her honesty. When moments passed without any comment, she settled back into her seat and fastened the seat belt.

Kyle fastened his seat belt and reached for Rudy's cell phone. He handed it to her before starting the Jeep and pulling back onto the highway. His attitude didn't invite further confidences.

"Better call directory assistance and get the number for the Somerset police," he said. "Tell them where to find Rudy and that there might be a warrant for his arrest."

"What if he tells them we attacked him and stole the car? They might put out a warrant for us."

"He can't risk involving more law enforcement agencies. His only recourse right now is silence."

Rianna got the number and called the police department. She identified herself as FBI Agent Mary Sullivan, and gave them her shield number. Then she explained her belief that a wanted criminal could be located in the alley near the post office. She added a warning that Rudy was extremely dangerous and might have cohorts in the area.

"Done," she said as she clicked off the connection.

"Did he sound podunk or professional?"

"He sounded skeptical, but intelligent and willing to follow through."

Next, she dialed Sullivan's private number. He answered after the first ring.

"What the hell took you so long to call?"

His impatience brought a smile to Rianna's lips. "We've been a little busy." She briefly outlined their escape from the boat, the electronic bug and the run-in with Rudy.

"He's still tied up in an alley?"

"I just reported him to the Somerset Police Department. You might want to call them and corroborate my story. There is a warrant for his arrest, isn't there?"

"Damn straight. And we have Haroldson behind bars." His tone held deep satisfaction. "He's been denied bail, at least for right now. I'm hoping the bulk of evidence will prevent any judge from releasing him, but you can bet his lawyers are working overtime to get him freed."

"Yes!" she shouted, feeling a rush of triumph. She turned to Kyle and repeated the good news. "He's behind bars and denied bail!" Of Sullivan, she asked, "You found the videotapes?"

"All of them, plus a few more stashed in the hidden safe you told me about. The evidence is damning and indisputable."

"You're being especially careful?"

"I swear on my life. He's not gonna slip through any legal loopholes. We've got him, and he's gonna pay, thanks to you."

"No." Rianna shook her head, thinking about her father and all the others who'd lost their lives. "Not just me. So many people gave so much. They all deserve credit."

"Where are you now?"

She glanced at Kyle, wondering how much to say over the phone. "I'm not on a secure phone. We took this one from Rudy, so I'd better leave details 'til later. When do you need me in D.C.?"

"We'll need depositions as soon as possible. You know the drill. I'd like to get started Monday. Make your way back to the summer place this weekend, and we'll take it from there."

"Okay. I'll see you soon."

"Stay safe," Sullivan insisted, then broke the connection.

Rianna closed the phone and set it on the seat between her and Kyle. She briefly repeated the conversation to him even though he'd heard her end of it.

"Where's the summer place?"

"He has a cabin about an hour from D.C."

"You've been there?"

She shot a glance at him. His expression hadn't softened, and he sounded disgusted again. "I know how to get there." Her answer might not satisfy him, but she didn't want to deal with any more issues tonight.

Realizing she'd gotten really warm, she shut off the heater. "You can open a window if you want. I'm fine now."

"You're sure?"

"I'm sure." She tugged at the strap around her throat. "I'm hot now and this stupid collar is starting to strangle me. Where are we, anyway?"

She desperately wanted to believe they could outrun Gregory's lethal pursuit and make it to somewhere, anywhere safe.

Chapter 8

The ER doctor in Lexington ordered Kyle out of the room when he got ready to operate on Rianna, but Kyle refused to budge. He wouldn't leave her. Not even for a minute.

The last time he'd let her out of his sight, Rudy had grabbed her. He'd died a thousand deaths while that gun barrel was pressed against her face, and never wanted to feel that kind of fear again. Especially since the short-lived incident had triggered a violent reaction in her. She'd been handling her extraction from the undercover assignment in a safe, gradual manner until that point.

The doctor hadn't put up much of an argument once he'd introduced himself as Rianna's federal bodyguard. Fortunately, the doc had been so appalled by the implant that he'd removed it without asking a lot of questions. They'd gotten by with a minimum of detail.

The procedure only required local anesthetic and a

couple of new stitches. The operation was over in less than an hour with the whole visit charged to the FBI through Rianna's real bureau identification, Mary Sullivan.

"You're sure you feel like leaving the hospital so soon?" Kyle asked, sliding an arm around her back and guiding her out the emergency room doors. They'd decided to leave the Jeep in the hospital parking lot and hire a taxi. Tomorrow, they'd rent a different vehicle.

"I'm sure," she said. "There's no reason for me to stay. It's no different than any other outpatient surgery. Besides, Gregory had the bug implanted while I was in his house." Her tone turned caustic. "He didn't even bother with antibiotics."

Kyle's hands clenched into fists. He hated the idea of that scum touching her or having any control over her, whether they'd been intimate or not.

Endangering her with a less-than-sterile surgery was just one of Haroldson's many crimes. Inserting a foreign body so close to the base of her brain without her consent would be cause for prosecution in most people's eyes. The man had a lifetime of atrocities to atone for.

He couldn't think about it now. He had more immediate worries, like keeping Rianna safe. Just the thought made his gut twist. Somewhere along the line, she'd become more than an assignment; more than his need to avenge a partner's murder; more than just a friend. He hadn't worked it all out in his mind yet, but he was fully committed to protecting her from harm.

The taxi driver took them to a twenty-four-hour shopping mart where they had a bite to eat and bought a few necessities. Then they hired a different cab to take them to a motel on the north side of the city. It was nearing four a.m. by the time they'd registered and settled in to their room.

"Why don't you get cleaned up first," he told her after they'd done a complete security check, double-locking the door and window. The ground-level room was furnished in neutral tones like thousands of others in the chain—generic but clean.

"Suits me fine," said Rianna.

Kyle could see the strain of the day's events etched on her features. The fine skin under her eyes looked bruised and her face creased with worry lines. He had an unexpected urge to smooth away the creases and bring back her confidence.

"You're not supposed to get those stitches wet," he reminded, as she grabbed a shopping bag and walked into the bathroom.

"I know, and my hair's filthy. I'll have to improvise."

"Need help?"

His offer was sincere, yet the vision that popped into his mind was anything but pure. His memory conjured the image of her stretched out on a deck chair, her slim, shapely body glistening in the sun. Then he mentally removed the bikini—and felt a shaft of heat between his legs.

"No, thanks. I'll just be slow and careful."

Her calm rejoinder was further evidence of her exhaustion. She didn't even bother to berate him for the suggestion. Kyle smiled slightly, blocking the mental image and commanding his body to relax.

To pass the time, he sorted through the things he'd bought at the store: jeans, a couple of T-shirts and some underwear. The shoes he'd found at the cabin would be okay until he got home. He'd bought another pair of gym shorts for sleeping.

The only room available so late had been a single with a queen-size bed. That meant they'd have to share, and he'd have to make a strong effort to control his desire. A desire that had been steadily escalating since the first time he held the elusive Phantom in his arms.

Kicking off his shoes, he stretched out on the bed and grabbed the TV remote. The late-night offerings didn't hold much appeal, but he settled on the sports network to pass the time while he waited for his turn in the bathroom.

In less than fifteen minutes, the door reopened, and Rianna came back into the room. His breath stopped at the sight of her, his muscles knotting and slow heat curling in his belly.

The sleepwear she'd picked looked like a man's boxer shorts and a sleeveless white undershirt. It should have been plain, but not with the soft fabric molded to her damp body. She lifted an arm to adjust the towel around her head, and the action brought the shirt tight against the fullness of her breasts. She wore a bra, yet he could still see the outline of hard, round nipples.

Heat poured through him like roiling lava, slow and thick and scalding. A cloud of sweet-smelling steam engulfed him, making his muscles tighten even more, while his heart pumped a little too fast.

It would never do. They were both too tired to deal with sexual complications right now. Their relationship was too fragile, their future too unpredictable. Maybe a really cold shower would help.

Gritting his teeth, he clicked off the TV and rose from the bed. "You done in there?"

"It's all yours, but I could use a little help first, if you don't mind."

Kyle moved closer. Everything about her delighted his senses, so he feasted on the closeness. He wanted to touch and taste and explore. More important, he wanted to do anything he could to help her rest and recuperate from her ordeal.

"What's the problem?"

Her expression, though still weary, was relaxed. The delicate, freshly scrubbed features appealed to him far more than the perfectly made-up socialite demeanor. Everything about her attracted him like a magnet.

"I got my Band-Aid a little damp, so I took it off. Could you please put another one over the stitches?"

She handed him a fresh one and turned her back. His hands trembled as he applied it over the spot on her nape. Just the feel of her skin under his fingers sent erotic messages throughout his body, and had him aching for more. He dragged in a long breath, but that only served to pull her scent more deeply into his system.

"All set." He cleared the gruffness from his throat and grabbed some clean clothes. "I won't be long."

In actuality, it took him fifteen minutes of frigid water to calm his rampaging desire. Then he took his time shaving, brushing his teeth and drying his hair.

He hoped Rianna would be sound asleep by the time he returned to the bedroom, but no such luck. She sat at the top of the bed with her legs curled under her. Her hair framed her face in a perfect oval, the baby-fine tresses looking shiny, clean and soft. Her shorts and top did little to conceal all her tempting curves. The sight of her elevated his temperature again, to dangerous levels.

She gave him a gentle smile that sent his blood pressure soaring with the simple innocence of it. There was nothing sexual or deliberately alluring about her manner, and he didn't know if he liked that or not. He wanted her trust and wanted her to feel safe with him, but he didn't want things to get too platonic between them.

"Watching anything special or ready for some shut-eye?"

"Sleep," Rianna assured him, clicking off the television. She set the remote on the bedside table and switched off the light. Then she slid beneath the sheet.

"Okay if I sleep on the left side?"

"No problem," he said. "I'll leave the bathroom light on and keep the door cracked in case you have to get up during the night."

"Thanks."

Kyle laid the Glock on the table next to his side of the bed. He was certain Rianna had the smaller gun within reach. He didn't expect any trouble, but they couldn't afford to get careless.

He wondered what she'd done about her little security pouch. She obviously wasn't wearing the neon-green bikini anymore or he'd have seen it through her white shorts. Warning himself not to dwell on that area of her body, he switched off his light. Then he stretched out on top of the covers and folded his arms behind his head.

They lay quietly for a while, adjusting to the unfamiliar sounds and shadows. Kyle tried to concentrate on everything but the warm, sexy, sweet-smelling woman at his side and how long it had been since he'd shared a bed with any woman. He thought back to the night Sullivan had called him. He'd been wishing for a woman in his bed. Now he had one, but had to curb his appetite.

He listened to the steady hum of the air conditioner. It drowned out most of the noise beyond the room. He studied the sprinkler system valve on the ceiling, trying to keep his mind occupied until boring details could lull him to sleep.

"Kyle?"

Rianna's soft, hesitant whisper of his name made his nerves go haywire. He dragged in a slow breath.

"Yeah?"

She waited so long to respond that he finally shifted on his side and faced her. She turned toward him, her gaze settling on his face, but she didn't say anything else.

"What's wrong?"

"Would you hold me?"

A wild surge of emotion exploded inside him, so strong that it sent a shudder through his body. He wanted her in every sense of the word, in every way a man could want a woman, but he knew she only needed reassurance. She wasn't asking for sex, just comfort and the intimacy of being close to another human being.

Still, he didn't hesitate. He gathered her, sheet and all, into his arms and pulled her against his chest. She slid one arm around his waist and snuggled her face into the curve of his shoulder. Pressing a light kiss on the silky softness of her hair, he urged her to relax.

"You need to rest."

"I can't seem to shut down my brain."

He slowly rubbed the small of her back, enjoying the contact, even through layers of clothes. "You're not still worried about Haroldson's men?"

"No."

"Then what's bothering you? Something specific or just everything?" he asked, keeping his tone light.

"All of it. The ugliness and deceit and my part in it. Even though I know how important it was to bring him to justice, I wish I'd never heard his name. Never learned all his dirty secrets. Never had to deal with him."

Kyle went still. "Did he hurt you? Does he have some sort of sick or perverted habits?"

"No. I was just another possession."

Anger roared through him, swift and uncontrollable. "How the hell could you stand it? Seeing him every day? Living in his pocket? Letting him believe he had the right to touch you whenever he wanted?"

Rianna stiffened and started to pull from his grip, but Kyle instantly tightened his hold on her. He cursed his own lack of control and willed himself to calm down, willed his muscles to relax until she felt comfortable enough to continue.

"Sorry."

"I understand," she whispered, hugging him briefly. "It makes me sick with anger, too, but I've spent half my lifetime working toward one goal. I want to see him pay for his crimes. Every time I felt sickened by the sight of him, I reminded myself of those long, lonely years."

"Long and lonely?" He didn't understand. "Explain."

When she didn't immediately respond, he tilted her head so that he could look into her eyes. Even in the darkness, he could see the turbulent emotion.

"Why was it so important for you to bring him to

justice? He's just one of a thousand criminals the FBI wants.''

It took a few moments for her to answer, and he had to strain to hear the response.

''He killed my family.''

The cold, hard edge to her voice shook him as much as the bald statement. He knew he wasn't going to like the details, but he wanted her to trust him enough to offer them. Tucking her against his chest again, he murmured in her ear.

''Can you tell me about it?''

''I've never discussed it with anyone but Donald.''

A spike of jealousy caught him unaware, slamming through his body and making his muscles bunch. More slow, deep breaths.

''So tell me.''

A long minute passed. Rianna stroked his back, her hand soft and warm. He didn't know if she was searching for words or refusing to share the story, until she finally responded.

''My dad worked for Gregory a long time ago. As his accountant, Dad was the first to notice the money laundering and other illegal activities. He went to the FBI and agreed to testify, but Gregory managed to lay the blame on one of his bank managers. The charges against him were dropped.''

''Leaving your dad to pay the consequences?'' he put in grimly.

''Our family went into the protection program, but Gregory never stopped searching for us. He had to set an example, he had a reputation to establish, and he wanted revenge. We kept moving, but he kept finding us. When I was sixteen, his men shot both my parents and my baby brother. Then they set our house on fire, and it was all my fault,'' she ended on a sob.

"You can't blame yourself," he said gruffly. "You weren't responsible for his crimes."

Rianna continued in a strained voice. "It was my fault he found us again. Dad and Mom were worried and ready to move, but I had a date for the high school prom. I begged them to wait a few more days, and they only stayed because of me," she said roughly. "They'd have been safe if I hadn't been so spoiled and selfish."

Kyle's heart ached for her. He hugged her closer, wanting to absorb some of her pain. He knew how much it had hurt to lose his dad, then Margie. He could only imagine how Rianna had suffered. She'd lost everyone she loved, and she blamed herself.

"How'd you escape?"

She cleared her throat and continued in a flat tone. "I was at a neighbor's, but ran home when I heard the sirens. I'd been told to hide and call Donald in an emergency, so that's what I did. He falsified the records to show that I'd died, too, and then put me in protection again."

She didn't need to say any more. Kyle could figure out what had happened from that point. She'd become obsessed with the need to avenge her family, to see some form of justice done. Then she'd spent more than a decade working toward her most important assignment.

"You've got him now."

"He needs to pay for destroying my family."

Her breath caught on a strangled sob that made him ache to ease the pain. How could you comfort someone who'd lost so much? He still hadn't come to terms with the guilt over Margie's death. Rianna had lost her family, plus the innocence of youth. No wonder she was driven.

"Your family would be proud."

"You think?" she asked wistfully. "I wonder sometimes. My parents wanted to see Gregory brought to justice, but I'm not sure they'd approve of my methods. They'd never condone lying and deceit. I just didn't know any other way."

"How could they not be proud of your dedication and determination? You're working on the side of the law. That's the lesson they taught you."

She sighed, snuggling closer. "You're right. I followed in my dad's footsteps when I gave evidence to the FBI. And I'll testify just like he did, but I'm sick and tired of it. Once Gregory is convicted, I never want to hear his name again."

"I'll second that." He swore softly. "I don't care if I never hear the name again, either."

With those words, the conversation ended and the room grew quiet again.

"We'd better get some sleep," he finally murmured.

Rianna made a soft sound that could have been agreement, and then exhaustion took its toll. Her grip on his waist eased, and Kyle knew she'd finally drifted to sleep. He smiled slightly and dropped another kiss on her hair. The soft, silky feel of it soothed him as much as the warmth of her womanly body.

She generated a whole host of feelings he'd never experienced with any other woman, possessiveness being primary. He wanted to lay claim to her in the most elemental fashion, make love to her until she forgot every other man she'd ever known. Until her world revolved around him, not Haroldson, her job or anything else.

It was a selfish desire, but he felt it nonetheless. The admission made him frown. He'd never been the jealous, possessive type, had never wanted a woman to be solely dependent on him.

Rianna was different.

And definitely off-limits right now. He had to be patient. This wasn't the time or place to stake a claim. They both needed sleep. He pressed his cheek against the softness of hers and gradually let his mind and body relax.

Hours later, he awakened as the warmth of Rianna's body left his side. Grumbling in complaint, he reached for her, but she dodged his arms. He struggled with grogginess as she moved to the foot of the bed, pulling the sheet with her.

When she grasped one of his feet in her hands, her touch jarred him awake.

"What?"

He had no concept of the time, though sunshine glistened around the edges of the heavy drapes. The room was still shadowed, but light enough to see his sexy bedmate as she knelt at his feet. Her hair was tousled, her face flushed with sleep, and her expression mysterious.

She took his right foot into her hands and slowly massaged his heel, then his arch and the ball of his foot. Her hands were warm and soft, her thumbs stroking firmly. Heat arrowed up his leg to his groin. By the time she reached for his other foot, his morning arousal had surged to aching fullness.

"I owe you a massage," she said quietly, her gaze locking with his. "Remember?"

His voice came roughly. "You don't owe me anything."

He wanted her more than his next breath. The blood sang through his veins in a heated rush, but he didn't want her offering anything out of gratitude.

"You carried me too far. You'll be stiff and sore this morning." She moved between his legs and began to rub his right calf with long, strong strokes, her fingers working magic on the hard muscles. She gave the same slow, diligent attention to his left leg, and then both knees.

Kyle groaned with pleasure. "Damn, that feels good," he muttered, holding her gaze. They stared into each other's eyes for a long, breathless moment.

"Be warned," he told her softly. "If you keep it up, I'll want a whole lot more than a massage."

"I'll do my best," she promised huskily.

He gave her a fierce frown. "Not from gratitude." He didn't want gratuitous sex. He wanted her as needy as him.

She smiled, a slow, sultry, beautiful smile that turned his insides to mush and made his flesh prickle with anticipation.

"The massage is in appreciation. Anything else will be strictly my pleasure."

She trusted him. He'd finally earned her trust, and he knew it wasn't something she gave lightly. He hadn't realized how badly he wanted it until she offered it. Satisfaction flowed over him like warm honey.

Her palms flattened across the top of his thighs, her fingers still kneading. She spread his legs wider and inched closer. Her touch electrified him, the heat sizzling along his nerves, his muscles clenching with each new stoke.

When she slid her fingers toward the hem of his shorts, he shuddered and reached for her. She countered the move by grabbing his hands, pressing them on the bed and clucking her tongue in rebuke. Then she urged him to roll onto his stomach.

Kyle complied, turning, and muffled a moan against the pillow as she straddled his hips. Her heat seared him, her thighs blanketing him with feminine softness through the thin barrier of clothing. Blood roared in his head.

She worked on the muscles of his back and shoulders, her touch strong and sure. His hands curled into fists at his sides as his body sang with excitement. Next, she slowly slid off his hips and straddled his thighs.

"You're a little tense, Tremont," she teased.

His tone was hoarse with arousal. "No kidding."

Then her hands cupped his buttocks, strong fingers igniting an even stronger reaction from his flesh. His nerves were strung taut, his muscles bunched, his arousal growing thicker and harder with every beat of his heart.

Rianna slid off his legs and urged him to turn onto his back again. This time she straddled his hips, pressing her soft warmth tightly against his straining flesh. He made a sound deep in his throat and reached for her, but she snatched his hands and pressed them down on either side of his head. He tried to steal a kiss while she nibbled on his chin.

Her next caress was a string of wet, open-mouth kisses down his neck and across his chest. She took a long, torturous time to bathe his nipples. Her tongue sent hot, primitive need racing through him. Every nerve ending in his body hummed with tension.

By the time she'd worked her way down to his navel, his breathing had grown ragged and his chest heaved. He broke a sweat as her nimble fingers reached inside his shorts.

"You're killin' me," he groaned.

She cupped him and stroked him until Kyle nearly strangled on his own need. He couldn't let her fondle him much longer. This time when he reached for her, she didn't resist, but slid back up his body and locked her mouth with his.

Their moans mingled as he plunged his tongue through her lips and explored the sweet depths beyond. He wanted to taste every inch of her, eat her up and lose himself in the taste, scent and feel of her.

He cupped her head in his hands, clutching fistfuls of silky hair to guide her closer. Their mouths were pressed tightly together, but he still couldn't get enough of her. He angled his head, then sucked her tongue between his teeth and molded it with his own.

His hunger for her was insatiable. The more she gave, the more he wanted. He'd never wanted anyone so desperately. Even the need for breath annoyed him. After a quick drag of air, he captured her mouth in another deep, drugging kiss.

While he clung to her head, her hands were busy tugging at the waistband of his shorts. He paused long enough to shrug out of his clothes and kick them aside. Then he helped her lift her shirt over her head.

When she unhooked her bra and removed it, he was awed at her beauty. He forced himself to take long, calming breaths while he admired the feel and shape of her. He slid his palms over her rib cage and cupped the soft, firm mounds of her breasts, using his thumbs to bring the tips to rigid attention. She rocked against him in response, and her mewing sounds of pleasure fed his excitement.

"Kyle!"

The sound of his name on her lips had desire coiling even tighter in his groin. He pulled her up his body until he could replace his hand with his lips, and then sucked a nipple deeply into his mouth. He teased the tight bud with the tip of his tongue and felt her body arching against him in feminine demand.

Her throaty sound of hunger made him quiver like a tightly plucked bowstring. Together, they managed to get her out of her shorts and panties. Then they swallowed each other's groans as they savored the feel of bare flesh against bare flesh.

He clutched her thighs and bucked against her as they got lost in another potent, probing kiss. He felt her hands on his cheeks, her grasp tight. Her mouth grew demanding as she rubbed her breasts against his chest, the hard nubs of her nipples spiking the heat in him even higher.

They kissed until neither of them could breathe. Their chests heaved, their bodies straining for more. Then Rianna slid down his body until his straining arousal was trapped at the cradle of her thighs. He gasped for breath, his chest heaving at the exquisite feel of her.

"Protection?" she insisted throatily.

"In the drawer," he muttered.

She took care of that, too, and he almost came apart at her touch. Before he could completely recover, she eased herself onto his straining flesh and enveloped him with her soft, wet warmth.

So tight. So damn hot and tight. And so tense. It

took a minute, but he finally realized that she'd gone really still and tense.

"Rianna?"

"I'm okay," she whispered, but she still didn't move.

"What do you mean, 'okay'?" He didn't like the sound of it or her stillness. "It's been a while for you?" That would explain the incredible tightness.

She mumbled something he couldn't understand, and then an amazing thought struck him. "Please don't tell me this is your first time."

"Okay."

Her lack of denial sent a shudder through him and convinced him that he'd hit on the truth. A deep, possessive thrill coursed through him, quickly followed by a desperate need to be gentle.

He closed his eyes and groaned, but held completely still until she'd had time to adjust to the size and feel of him. She gripped him tightly, sending another quiver of erotic pleasure up his spine. Once she'd accepted him and begun to move, he grasped her hips, arching upward to meet her slow, careful thrusts.

The pressure built too quickly, the need too forceful. He strained to hold back, until Rianna moaned his name. Then he surged against her and felt himself exploding in one long, fierce burst of pleasure.

She collapsed against him, their chests heaving from exertion, the sound of their labored breathing filling the silence. He knew it hadn't been all that great for her, but he silently swore to make it up to her.

For the next few minutes, all they could do was fight for air and hold each other while they recovered from the emotional and physical high.

Kyle hugged her tightly, wanting to prolong the exquisite contact. He closed his eyes, relishing the shared intimacy and the gift she'd given him. Not just her body, but her trust. He knew she didn't give either one too freely. He'd made love to his share of women, but never to one who'd been as generous in her loving. Gut instinct told him what a treasure he'd found. She was his now, and he intended to keep her.

His partner.

His lover.

His woman.

Chapter 9

"**W**ow." Rianna exclaimed in a soft, sighing whisper. She'd never shared anything so intimate, but she could understand why women enjoyed it so much.

Their chests had stopped heaving, but his vibrated again with triumphant male laughter.

"'Wow' doesn't even come close," he argued gruffly. "It gets a lot better, I promise."

That brought a smile of satisfaction to her lips. She'd wanted their loving to be incredibly special because that's how she felt about him—a special, unique feeling unlike anything she'd ever known with a man.

His response thrilled her and sounded so sincere that she pressed a hard kiss on his chest.

"Control yourself, woman," he teased, running his fingers through her hair.

Then he cupped her head with his palm and lifted her face for a long, sweet kiss. She gently sucked his tongue into her mouth until a low, hungry sound gurgled from his throat.

When their lips parted, their gazes tangled. They stared into each other's eyes, intently searching. Rianna wondered what he hoped to find in hers. The dark, possessive gleam in his sent a tremble over her. Her nipples tightened in reaction. Their bodies were still so closely entwined that she felt his muscles begin to twitch with renewed energy.

"You should have told me," he insisted.

She didn't want to discuss her virginity or make a big deal of it. Nor did she want to tell him that he was the first man who'd ever tempted her to part with it.

"I'm the one who did the seducing," she reminded.

He wasn't satisfied with her response. He started to speak, but she placed a hand over his mouth. "We have to get moving." She wanted nothing more than to spend the day, or several, in bed in his arms. There was so much about him that she still needed to explore.

Kyle lifted his arm to check his watch. "It's after eleven and we have to be out of here by noon."

He didn't mention that Gregory's men might have tracked down Rudy and the rented Jeep by now. Given enough time, they'd eventually find them.

Rianna sighed. "First dibs on the bathroom," she said, wondering how to gracefully extricate herself from their embrace. Even though they'd just shared an incredible intimacy, she suddenly felt shy and awkward. She had no experience to fall back on, and modesty had her searching for something to cover herself.

"How about we share a shower? It'll save time," said Kyle.

She blinked, and then studied his wickedly suggestive expression. His eyes had that hungry look again.

Her stomach muscles clenched, but she had to resist temptation.

"You don't really think that will save time, do you?" she admonished, laughing and wedging some space between their upper bodies.

"It could happen."

When she started to sit up, he cupped her breasts in his hands. The contrast between his deeply tanned skin and her pale flesh gave her a feminine thrill. She watched him watching her as her breasts swelled, the tips budding. He teased them to hardness. When she felt his body hardening within hers, she cried out softly.

"Kyle!"

He held her gaze. "I know, we have to go, and you can't take a shower. You can't get your neck wet. But we could share a quick bath."

So sexy. So much a man. He was so handsome and irresistible that Rianna felt herself melting all over again. She barely recognized her own throaty voice when she finally managed a response.

"A bath sounds nice."

Kyle twisted around until his feet hit the floor, then he grasped her hips, lifting her without withdrawing from her body. She gasped at the exquisite sensation that coursed through her. His strength and obvious desire stirred hers to a frenzy again.

"Gun and condom," he mumbled as he locked his mouth on her neck, sucking strongly, drawing another gurgle of approval from deep in her throat.

Rianna grabbed both from the bedside stand, then wrapped her arms around his shoulders, rubbing her breasts against his chest to ease their tight ache.

She locked the door behind them once they'd entered the bathroom, then scattered kisses over his chest while he reached down to turn on the faucets. They paused for a long kiss as water filled the tub and steam began to fill the room.

Kyle laid the gun on the soap shelf, took care of protection and brought his hands back to her buttocks. He cupped her with his big palms, squeezing gently, then more roughly as sharp, heated passion flared between them again. He clutched her closer. She rocked against him in demand, and then swallowed his low growl.

She felt the heavy thrust of his hips as he began to move deep inside of her with renewed fervor. The fire in her belly flared like a torch to kindling. She wanted him closer, deeper. She wanted him so close that he became an extension of herself.

He turned, pressing her back against the wall so that he could free a hand to grasp her head. Then he plunged his tongue into her mouth, demanding another deep, wet, devouring kiss.

Rianna's thighs clenched convulsively, and she hugged him with arms and legs as he rocked against her. She returned his hungry kisses while meeting him thrust for powerful thrust, until they exploded in another fierce eruption of pleasure.

Guttural sighs of completion mingled in their mouths. When Kyle finally broke the contact, he pressed his forehead against hers. They sagged against the wall, trembling from head to toe, momentarily exhausted. Their breathing was labored again, with each fighting to draw air into depleted lungs.

''Whew!'' he exclaimed on a harshly exhaled breath.

Rianna didn't even have the strength to laugh. She gave him a shaky smile, then a light kiss on the nose.

She clung to his sweat-slick body with what little strength she had left in hers.

He tightened his hold on her again, turning toward the tub. After testing the temperature, he shut off the taps and slowly eased her into the water. She tried to tug him in with her, but he resisted.

"Better not," he said, his voice still rough, his eyes glazed with satisfaction. He pressed a hard kiss to her lips, then drew in a rough breath and continued. "We'll have an overflow and end up wasting more time."

Rianna knew he was right. She reluctantly released him, then immediately felt naked and exposed. As soon as he'd moved back a step, she pulled the curtain to block his view.

"Hey!" he complained.

"I'm shy," she responded, grabbing a washcloth and soap.

His sexy laughter echoed in the small room. "You'll get over it," he promised.

She smiled to herself, but wondered at his assurances. Would she get the chance to grow accustomed to Kyle's loving? Would there ever be time and opportunity to make love until they were totally comfortable with each other? She doubted it, and it scared her to want it so badly.

As soon as he was out of sight, doubts started to assail her. For years, the only future she'd considered was the successful completion of this assignment. She hadn't allowed herself to think beyond that goal.

She had never allowed herself to become emotionally involved with a man. Never allowed herself to care so much, so fast. Had she just risked their lives by tempting fate? In her life, caring too much meant inviting pain and heartache.

One thing was certain. They had to concentrate on getting back to D.C. She couldn't fail now. She couldn't worry about relationships or the future or anything other than bringing Gregory Haroldson to justice. Everything else had to be put on hold until she'd accomplished that objective. She needed to stay focused, but it was getting harder and harder to do, with Kyle so near.

He shaved while she finished bathing, then they switched places. By the time he'd finished showering, she'd dressed in jeans and a yellow T-shirt. She was getting really tired of stiff, itchy new clothes, but didn't have much choice. Soon she'd be home and could get comfortable again.

Just a few more hours.

Then what? What would happen when she no longer needed Kyle's protection? When his promise to Donald had been fulfilled and their extraordinary partnership dissolved? Would that be the end of it? Would he go home, get on with his life and chalk up their time together as just one final assignment to be forgotten?

It hurt to even think about the what-ifs.

And that scared her spitless. The hurting part. She'd had more than her fair share of hurting. She'd been so careful not to care too much about anyone, yet Kyle had sneaked past her guard. He'd crept into her wary heart while she'd been too busy staying alive to notice the risk.

She couldn't worry about it now. They had to get back to Virginia. Their best hope was that Donald had all Gregory's men rounded up by now. Rudy should still be in jail, but they couldn't relax until Tabone, Damon and the others were accounted for. Not to mention anyone in the agency who remained on Gregory's payroll.

Rianna sat down on the bed and started pulling on her shoes, but when the bathroom door opened, her gaze flew to it. She caught her breath at the sight of Kyle, still damp from his shower, wearing nothing but a towel hitched around his waist.

Gorgeous didn't even come close to describing him. Extremely sexy. Incredibly virile. Unbearably appealing. His sun-bronzed skin glistened over broad shoulders, a muscled chest and flat stomach. Silvery-blond hair curled between dark nipples and arrowed downward toward the low-slung towel. Her blood began to heat all over again.

He returned her stare with equal intensity until the emotion flowing between them became almost too painful to bear. Panic clutched at her chest and climbed into her throat.

Her brave, sexy lover was also one of the most honorable men she'd ever known. That thought crowded out his physical appeal and reminded her that she'd complicated his life, endangered it, and made him an unwilling accomplice to the nightmare she'd been living for months.

"What's wrong?"

She shook her head and dropped her gaze, then concentrated on tying her shoes.

"Rianna?"

He started toward her, but she rose and put out a hand to halt him.

He frowned. "You're not sorry…"

"No!"

Her emphatic response seemed to reassure him. He

gave her a smile and she returned it with one of her own.

"You're sure?" he demanded.

"Positive."

He studied her for another few seconds. "Good," he said. "I don't want you to have any regrets."

When she gave her head a vigorous shake, he finally turned away and started pulling clothes out of shopping bags.

She tried to lighten the mood. "I'm just worrying again," she said, moving toward the window to peek out the curtain. "Everything looks quiet, and there's only one car in the parking lot. We're probably the last to leave."

"Yeah, I imagine most of their customers are vacation travelers. Everyone else probably got an early start."

Rianna kept her gaze on the parking lot, but her attention stayed on Kyle. She heard him pulling on his shorts, then jeans, the zipper sounding especially loud in the quiet of the room. When he tugged a white T-shirt over his head, she turned to watch the flex of muscles as he tucked in his shirt and fastened the snap of his jeans.

Everything he did, every move he made, fascinated her. She wanted more time to explore, wanted to sate herself with him and then start all over again. Her heart pounded painfully in her chest at the idea of unrestrained, uninhibited loving.

Until today, she'd never thought of herself as a particularly sensual woman, but he'd changed that image forever. She wanted to smell and taste and feel until she had her fill. Just a pipe dream at this point in her life.

"Rianna? You sure you're okay?"

She realized she was staring at him again, and licked her suddenly dry lips. "To be honest, I'm having a little withdrawal here. I want to go back to bed with you and stay there for a long, long time."

She could see the effect her honesty had on him. His eyes darkened, his jaw tightened and his hands clenched into fists at his sides. His whole body went tense, then he took a deep breath and slowly exhaled.

"Someday soon," he swore softly.

She forced herself to breathe deeply, too. "I'm going to hold you to that, Tremont."

He grinned, a purely male, purely wicked grin that lightened her spirits. "You won't have to work too hard at it."

"Promise?"

"On my life."

She returned his grin, and then crossed the room to collect the small pistol from the nightstand. She stashed it in a leather fanny pack she'd bought at the store last night, added the plastic bag with the disabled electronic bug they'd smashed and bagged, along with the refrigerator magnet. It was further evidence of Gregory's treachery.

Kyle tucked the Glock into the waistband of his jeans and covered it with his shirt. They were ready again.

"What now? Rent a car and drive to D.C.? Or take a cab to the airport?"

"I vote for flying, but the airports would be the most likely place to look for us. Especially Dulles," she said.

"We could drive into Ohio and catch a flight to Newark, then rent a car. They can't watch every airport in the region."

Rianna nodded. "I want to call Donald again and get his input before deciding."

She could tell the idea didn't set well with Kyle. Why? Just a male thing, or a genuine mistrust of the other man? Surely that couldn't be the case. He was here as a favor to Donald.

"The fewer people who know our plans, the safer we'll be," he reminded.

"Donald may have news about Rudy and the others, and I want to make sure Gregory's still behind bars."

Kyle seemed reluctant, but finally nodded. "Okay, we call Sullivan, but not from Rudy's cellular. We'll bag it up with anything else we don't want and toss it in the Dumpster. We can find a pay phone to call Sullivan." He looked around. "Is that it?"

She'd already bagged up what few clothes she wanted to take with her and discarded the others. After surveying the room one last time, she nodded. "I don't think there's anything else."

"No extra underwear?" The frown on his face kicked up in a provocative grin. His blue eyes glittered like sapphires.

Rianna felt her face heat at the suggestion. "A good old safety pin will suffice in the absence of built-in panty pouches."

"Glad to hear it."

She'd forgotten to give him some money in case they got separated. Turning her back, she unfastened her jeans, unclipped the safety pin and pulled out a couple of big bills. When she'd refastened everything, she turned again, slamming into Kyle's chest.

The look on his face was so lascivious that she laughed out loud. "Back off, Tremont. You're altogether too interested in my secret hiding place."

"Damn straight," he growled, stealing a quick kiss.

Rianna returned his kiss with fervor, but they refrained from holding each other. When they broke apart, she handed him some money.

"First time I ever got paid for a kiss." He tucked the bills into his pocket.

"Consider it an advance," she teased.

"On services to be rendered?"

"Sounds good to me."

He made a move to take her into his arms, but quickly backed off. "Damn."

"I know." She felt the same way. She didn't want to leave their little cocoon and face the world again, but they had no real choice. "A cab or a rental company?"

"There's a little restaurant a couple of blocks down the street," he told her. "I noticed it last night. Why don't we walk down there, get something to eat, and see if any of Haroldson's men crawl out of the woodwork. If it looks safe, we can hire a cab to take us to the airport."

Rianna thought about it. Flying would certainly be the fastest way to make the trip. Kyle probably didn't want to waste any more time on the road dodging henchmen. He'd gone above and beyond his duty as a private citizen. He had to be anxious to get rid of her and get back to his normal life.

The idea shouldn't hurt, yet it did.

"Sounds like a plan." She hoped her tone sounded brisk and professional. It was time to start putting some emotional distance between them.

Turning from his probing gaze, she added, "I'm starved."

"Rianna?" He stopped her as she reached for the

doorknob. When she turned, he placed a brief, hard kiss on her lips, and then nudged her aside.

"I'll go first, make a sweep of the parking lot and toss our trash in the Dumpster. Then I'll check the office, and signal from there if it's all clear."

She sighed, but nodded agreement. As he made his way around the motel lot, she watched for any sign of trouble. She'd guarded the backs of other agents in the past, but never one that meant so much to her. She barely breathed until she saw him waving an all-clear from the doorway of the office. Quickly donning a pair of sunglasses, she joined him on the main sidewalk, where he put himself between her and the busy street.

The midday sun was hot, and their walk brisk. The street was lined with cars parked in front of various small shops. Two lanes of traffic moved steadily along, but no one seemed to pay them any undue attention. None of the passing vehicles held familiar faces or any sort of threat to them.

By the time they reached the restaurant, they were ready for the air-conditioning. Kyle settled into a corner booth with a clear view of the entrance and parking lot, while she made use of the pay phone just inside the front door.

She heard a series of clicks as Donald's home answering system forwarded her call. He picked up within a few seconds and didn't bother with polite greetings.

"Where are you?"

"We're in Lexington, and we want to fly back, but I wanted to make one last check with you before leaving here. What's happening?"

"Haroldson is still behind bars, but his lawyer is pulling out all the stops to get him freed. I convinced the police down there to keep Rudy until we can make a prisoner transfer.''

''Good. How about Tabone and the others?''

''I'm trying to verify their whereabouts, but they're still wild cards. Our best guess is they won't do anything too stupid or too public.''

''So you think it's safe for us to fly?''

''I don't advise it,'' he said. ''I don't have enough manpower to patrol the airports and there are too many of Haroldson's men unaccounted for. If you keep driving, you'll be one step ahead of them and leave a cold trail.''

Rianna didn't know how Kyle would take the news of more hours on the road, but she had to agree. She didn't like the odds of a busy airport. If they flew, they wouldn't have the authority to carry their weapons, so they'd be especially vulnerable.

Donald barely paused. ''You know the drill. Make sure you aren't being tailed, and head for the cabin. It's as secure as any safe house and you know the alarm codes. I should be there ahead of you, or as soon as I can get there.''

''It'll take us another eight or ten hours.''

Something in her tone had alerted him to her mood. ''Tremont giving you trouble?''

''No.''

''Your neck all right? You're not hurting?''

''No, I'm fine, really. I'm just ready to be home.''

''Soon,'' he reassured her. ''It's been the longest six months of my life, but I'll have you home soon. Then I'm never letting you out of my sight again.''

The fierceness of his tone made Rianna chuckle. ''Yes, sir,'' she teased. ''Suits me just fine.''

His voice dropped to a low murmur. "You know I love you."

"I know," she whispered. His unfaltering devotion had sustained her through some rough times. "I love you, too."

They said goodbye, and she returned to the booth. Kyle stared at her for a minute, his expression unexpectedly grim, and then he turned his attention to a menu.

She frowned, wondering what had caused his mood to darken, but she didn't ask. Instead, she studied her own menu. Once the waitress had taken their order and they were alone again, she outlined Donald's plan.

"I forgot we'd have to ditch our guns if we flew," he admitted, his brow furrowing. "Does Sullivan think Tabone and the others are still tailing us?"

"He can't be sure. They're unaccounted for, at this point. Damon's a wild card, too. I didn't have any concrete evidence against him, so he's not in custody. There's a warrant for Tabone if Donald finds him before he finds us."

"Let's hope he went into hiding when he heard about the other arrests."

"He's more of a lackey than a thinker, so he and the others might have given up the chase. With Gregory and Rudy in jail, there's no one left to organize the troops. At least, not for a while."

"I'm sure Haroldson has someone on payroll who's doing his bidding and seeing that his orders are obeyed."

"That would be Sanderson, his lawyer and flunky. He'll be the go-between for a while, but Donald is trying to freeze Gregory's assets. In that case, nobody gets paid."

"And a good crook's loyalty has to be bought."

"Right. If we spend another day on the road, all the rats will be abandoning ship."

Kyle gave her a strange look but didn't comment. Their meal arrived, so they were quiet while they ate. Despite being hungry, the food didn't sit well on Rianna's stomach.

Her thoughts churned while she considered the best way to handle the rest of the trip. She knew she needed to give him the opportunity of opting out of the mission, yet she hated to broach the subject. He'd be relieved or offended by her suggestion, and either option made her sick at heart.

When she'd eaten as much as she could manage, she studied Kyle for a minute, until the intensity of her scrutiny caught his attention.

"What's worrying you now?"

Rianna wasn't sure she liked having him read her mind or be so aware of her mood swings. She'd never had a truly intimate, sharing sort of relationship with a man who could sense her thoughts and feelings.

Avoiding the problem wouldn't solve it, so she explained. "I'm thinking it might be safer to go our separate ways now. If Gregory's men are still searching for us, they'll be looking for Tony and Samantha, not a lone woman who doesn't look very glamorous anymore."

Kyle's expression went stone cold. His lips thinned and his eyes glittered. The muscles in his jaw clenched, and she knew she'd really ticked him off. Part of her exalted in the knowledge while part of her cringed.

"Trying to give me my walking papers, Rianna?"

His tone rivaled the air-conditioning for chill factor. She fidgeted with her napkin. Then, annoyed with her uncharacteristic restlessness, she tossed it down and looked him directly in the eyes.

"I don't want you to feel obligated to drive all the way back to D.C. with me. I know you put your own life on hold to help Donald, but you've already done more than you bargained for. I think I'll be safe from here on out."

His expression went blank, his tone bland. "You think?"

She clenched her jaw, wishing she knew what he really wanted. "I'm a highly trained professional, remember?"

"Even the best professional needs backup sometimes." He watched her with unerring intensity. "What about the promise you just made? We have a lot of unfinished business between us."

"I'm not denying that," she said, lowering her lashes to hide how deeply his words touched her. "I'm just suggesting that it might have to wait until this whole case is settled."

"You don't think we make good traveling partners?"

She forced herself to look up at him again. "I'm more like a liability you haven't been able to shake. Not to mention you're risking your own life."

"If this is all about me, then why don't you let me decide if and when I want to be cut free?"

Relief rushed through her. She desperately wanted him to want to stay with her, but not out of some misguided sense of duty and honor. She took a deep breath and forced herself to relax.

"You think we can manage to stay one step ahead of the bad guys without risking life or limb?"

The tension in Kyle's expression eased at her attempt to dispel the dark mood, but his steady gaze didn't waver from her face. His tone was terse when he spoke again, his expression accusing.

"Was that a test, Special Agent Phantom?"

She blinked, disconcerted again by the way he read her thoughts and intentions. When she locked gazes with him again, hers was clear and steady. "Maybe a little one, but please don't be offended. I really want to do what's best for you at this point. You've put your own life on hold for a long time now."

He lifted a brow in arrogant disagreement. "How long have you been working the case?"

Rianna stared at him. She'd been undercover for a good part of the year, but she'd been working the case half her life. She shook her head, unwilling to voice the whole truth.

They were quiet for a minute, and then Kyle broke the silence with a new suggestion. "I think what's best for both of us is a little moving excursion."

She didn't follow his line of thinking. "What do you mean?"

He nodded toward the window facing the intersection. She followed his gaze, but didn't see anything out of the ordinary.

"What?"

"A truck rental company," he explained, pointing across the street. "Nobody's likely to be looking for us in a moving van. What do you say to renting one of those for the trip back east?"

She offered him a genuine grin. "Sounds like a winner. I still have one more phony ID to use."

His eyes darkened and his tone dropped an octave. "In your security pouch?"

She laughed out loud and then rose from the table. "In my jeans pocket, Tremont. My jeans pocket."

His answering grin warmed her heart.

Chapter 10

They rented a small panel van and Kyle took the first shift of driving. Rianna couldn't believe how exhausted she still felt. She dozed during the next few hours, interspersing her sleep with long conversations about his home in Texas and his woodcraft business.

She learned that after retiring from the agency, he'd worked as a security guard for a fast-growing company. His investment in the company's stock allowed him the financial freedom to work for himself. He'd developed a longtime love of woodworking into a small business that was just starting to earn a profit.

The more she learned about Kyle, the more her admiration for him grew. He knew who he was and what he wanted from life. He had a real home and a plan for his future. In comparison, hers seemed really bleak. She'd never allowed herself to dream of any life beyond her obsessive need to see Gregory Haroldson punished.

Once she'd accomplished that objective, she had no idea what she'd be doing. The future loomed big and empty, all her insecurities threatening to rear their ugly heads. Despite her confidence in her ability to do her job, she had little else to be confident about these days. She had no close friends, no relationship skills or long-term goals.

In other words, not much to offer any man. That depressing thought had alarm bells ringing in her head. She was getting in way over her head with the renegade retiree. He'd never mentioned anything about permanency or long-term commitments. They had only known each other a few days, even though it seemed so much longer.

They stopped for dinner in Charleston, West Virginia, and then Rianna took the wheel so that Kyle could get some rest. The freeway driving was monotonous, but uneventful, as they swapped places every couple of hours. The steady speed allowed them to make good time, and they reached Maryland a little before midnight. It took another hour to get to Donald's cabin.

The natural wood, A-frame house nestled atop a small hill in a copse of evergreen trees. It sat about a hundred yards from the road and was surrounded by aesthetically appealing, high-security fencing. Lights blazed, illuminating the house from several directions.

Rianna's heart skipped a beat as they approached the iron entrance gates. The cabin had become her second home over the past few years, and the thrill of being close delighted her beyond words. She gave Kyle the code, and the heavy gates silently slid apart for them to pass.

As soon as they pulled to a stop near the house, the

front door opened. Donald stepped onto the porch, a tall, distinguished man with thick, graying hair and a smile that lit his craggy, aristocratic features with happiness. Rianna threw open her door, hopping out of the van before Kyle turned off the engine.

In the next instant, she and Donald had narrowed the distance between them, and she threw herself into his waiting arms. He hugged her fiercely, and she returned the embrace with all her strength. Her chest tightened, her throat constricting at the feel of his solid strength. She'd missed him badly.

"Welcome home, baby," he whispered near her ear, tenderly rocking her back and forth.

"You can't imagine how great it is to be here!" she insisted, blinking back tears and fighting a landslide of emotion. It rolled over her with an intensity that had her trembling in his arms.

"It's been too long," he added gruffly, reassuring her. "It's okay now. You're home and you're safe. I can do all the worrying from here on out. You just relax."

"I'll be happy to," she said, easing a little space between them so she could study his familiar, ageless features. "I'm ready to be done with it."

Their quiet conversation was interrupted by Kyle's terse greeting to Donald. "Sullivan."

His cold, hard tone had them slowly pulling apart and turning toward him. He stood in the shadows, but the bright porch light shone on his dark, angry expression. His stance was combative, his hand folded around the Glock. Rianna was taken aback by his belligerent attitude. He looked like an gunfighter itching for a fight.

"Kyle?" Her tone was questioning, but he ignored her and continued to glare at Donald.

"Tremont." Donald returned the greeting. The arm around her waist tightened protectively.

"Rianna's too exposed out here." Kyle ground the words out roughly.

The two men continued to scowl at each other for a few seconds, and then Donald agreed. "You're right." He nudged her toward the doorway. "Let's get inside." To Rianna, he added, "Somebody else is a little anxious to see you."

She shrieked with excitement. "Sophie's here?"

"Against my better judgment, but you know she never listens to anything I say."

They'd barely stepped into the house and closed the door before Rianna was being wrapped tightly in another pair of arms. The women shared cries of joy at seeing each other again. Donald's wife added her enthusiastic welcome with motherly hugs and kisses.

When they'd quieted, Donald made introductions.

"Tremont, this is my wife, Sophie," he said with an amused lift of his brow. "Sophie, this is Kyle Tremont. You've heard me mention him in the past. He used to be one of my agents, but I don't think the two of you ever met."

The slim, attractive redhead freed one hand and reached it to him. He grasped it briefly and nodded in greeting.

"I'll never be able to thank you enough for bringing Mary safely back to us," she insisted.

The Sullivans had always used the abbreviated form of Marianna for security purposes. They'd wanted her to retain part of her identity without putting her at risk, so she'd been Mary to them. Just another of her many names.

"She's the daughter of our hearts, and we've been worried sick about her for months," Sophie explained.

Kyle's thunderous expression lightened, and Rianna belatedly realized he'd been jealous of Donald. Her eyes widened at his misconception. Did he think her that dense and insensitive?

She frowned, flashing him a chastising look.

He returned her glance with an arrogant arch of a brow and without apology.

Donald cleared his throat, and Sophie chuckled softly at the byplay. "Boys," she scolded. "None of that macho posturing. We're all adults here."

Rianna just shook her head in disbelief. She actually felt flattered by Kyle's possessive attitude, and she'd never have believed it possible. Maybe she was getting soft in the head.

Or the heart.

That errant thought made her frown. She'd never aspired to be softheaded or softhearted.

"How's your neck?" asked Donald. "Let me see."

Rianna slid her hand up to touch the tiny row of stitches.

"What's wrong with your neck?" Sophie asked in alarm. "Did somebody try to strangle you?"

"No, no," Rianna insisted, glancing at Donald for guidance. He gave her a subtle shake of his head. She didn't like lying to Sophie, so she kept her explanation to a minimal. "I got hurt and had to have a couple of stitches, but it's fine now."

Sophie frowned, glancing from one of them to the other. Noting their closed expressions, she made a clucking sound of disgust. "Okay, don't tell me. I'm sure it's classified. Just show me and let me decide if it's all right or not.''

Rianna turned her back, lifted her hair and tugged the Band-Aid off her neck. Sophie and Donald both shifted closer, studying the sutures. Sophie ran a gentle finger near the slightly raised flesh. Then they both conceded that the wound was healing nicely.

''Does it still hurt?'' asked Donald.

''It never hurt very much, but it's starting to itch.''

''That's just part of the healing process,'' chimed Sophie. ''Did you need a tetanus shot? Your last one is probably outdated. Are you on antibiotics?''

''The doctor gave me a tetanus booster and a few days' worth of antibiotics,'' Rianna lied, intent on calming her concern. Sophie worried too much over the small things because she knew she had no control over the life-threatening ones.

''But it's never felt like it might be infected,'' she added. ''It's really just a scratch.''

Sophie cleared her throat. ''Of course it is. Absolutely nothing to worry about. I promise I'm not going to waste time clucking over you like a mother hen.'' She quickly changed the subject. ''Are you hungry? Donald insists that I can only stay a couple of hours. Safety first and all that, but we have time to share a meal.''

''Something smells delicious,'' said Rianna.

''Your favorite, of course.'' Sophie hugged her close again. They led the way down the hall to the kitchen with the men following. ''Pot roast with new potatoes and baby carrots. I even outdid myself with dessert. Coconut cream pie with lots of tall, fluffy meringue.''

Rianna moaned in delight. ''You shouldn't have

gone to so much trouble, but I'm glad you did. My mouth's watering already.''

''Consider yourself lucky,'' Donald teased. ''My stomach's been growling loud enough for the neighbors to hear, but Sophie wouldn't give me a scrap of food until you got home.''

''My poor darling,'' Sophie cooed, wrinkling her nose at her husband. ''You do have it rough, don't you.''

Their good-natured teasing set the tone for the next hour. Everyone seemed determined to enjoy the meal without letting reality intrude. There was no mention of the ongoing case or anything serious until they'd finished eating.

Over coffee, Donald caught them up on the Haroldson matter. The overwhelming evidence against the man prevented him from using his money or power to influence the courts. None of his wealthy associates was willing to risk supporting him at this point. He was still being held without bond, and his lawyer was starting to discuss the possibility of cutting a deal.

''The district attorney has assured me that the state won't accept a plea bargain. Not unless it's from Rudy Barrick. If he wants to turn state's evidence against Haroldson, then they might bargain for reduced sentences, but nobody is walking in this case.''

''Is there any way Mary can avoid testifying?'' asked Sophie.

''As the agent assigned to the case, her testimony is crucial,'' Donald explained. ''I wish we could get by with a formal deposition, but her eyewitness accounts need to be heard by the judge and jury. We probably have enough evidence to lock Haroldson away for a few years, but her testimony can keep him behind bars with no chance of parole.''

''Couldn't she do one of those video testimonies?'' asked Sophie. ''Aren't they sometimes used to protect an agent's identity or safety?''

''The judge might allow it,'' he replied, his tone noncommittal. ''But it's not nearly as effective as putting her in the courtroom.''

''There could be years of appeals,'' said Kyle.

''I understood all that from the beginning,'' Rianna insisted, her tone firm. ''I'm totally committed to seeing the process to an end, however long it takes. I will not let him win this battle.''

Quiet settled over the room as they all accepted the reiteration of her decision. Then Kyle changed the subject. ''What have you learned about Blaine? How long's he been dirty?''

Before Donald could respond, Rianna added another question. ''Was he the mole who kept selling my family's whereabouts to Gregory?'' She'd vowed to learn who was responsible for the breach in security that had compromised her family's location every few years.

''I don't see how Blaine could have had access to that kind of high-level information,'' said Kyle.

''He didn't,'' explained Donald. ''When we searched Blaine's apartment, we found a ledger that belonged to my predecessor, Bob Mullet. Apparently Bob had been selling information to Haroldson for years.''

''Didn't Mullet die a few months after Margie?'' asked Kyle.

''Yeah, supposedly of natural causes, but we're checking into that a little closer now, too. From what we can determine, Blaine learned about Mullet's in-

volvement though Margie's death and started black-
mailing him. When Mullet died, Blaine offered himself
as Haroldson's new mole.''

''And now they're both gone.''

Rianna's comment brought silence to the room. The
new information went a long way toward answering
some unresolved issues regarding her family.

''I'm sure Haroldson is actively recruiting new in-
formants,'' said Donald. ''All we can hope for is to
stay one step ahead of him.''

''And we still don't know who actually killed my
parents and brother.''

''Mullet's records might give us another lead on that,
too,'' added Donald. ''There's a mention of a hired
gun. We think it relates to an international hit man, but
that's all we have to work with. No name or country
of origin.''

''So he could be dead or alive?''

''Anything's possible, but that was a long time ago
and it's not a very safe profession. Chances are he's
dead or serving time for another murder. Haroldson
isn't likely to cough up that kind of information, so we
might never know for certain.''

Rianna wished they could be sure. She desperately
wanted to put all the questions, all the worrying and
wondering behind her. She wanted to be able to remember her family without the pain, guilt and heartache. Thinking about them led to another question.

''Did you get the video I asked you to keep for me?
The personal one?'' she asked.

Donald smiled, his eyes lighting with pleasure. ''It's
in the living room. We noticed the date on the label,
and I can see why it's so important to you.''

She gave him a big smile. ''Thanks a bunch.''

To Kyle, she explained. "When I was searching through Gregory's tapes, I found a series of videos from his annual staff parties. My parents, brother and I are on one of them."

She cleared the thickness from her voice, wondering if she'd ever be able to speak of them without getting weepy. She'd lost everything in that fire, every personal item, photo and small memento of their family life.

"I couldn't risk watching it too much, so I hid it with the evidence tapes."

Their gazes met and held. His reassuring expression eased the tightness in her chest. For so many years, she'd been unable to mention her family to anyone but Donald and Sophie. Discussing them more openly now brought her an unexpected sense of comfort.

"You'll have to introduce me to them later," Kyle told her in quiet understanding.

His sensitivity brought a lump to her throat. She dropped her gaze to her coffee cup, and then took one last sip. Sophie had finished cleaning the kitchen while they talked. Donald shifted back into his deputy director mode.

"Can you stay a while longer, Tremont? At least until I get Sophie back to the city?"

Kyle nodded, and Donald continued. "I'll take the rented truck and follow her back to our apartment. My car's in the garage in case of emergency, along with the pickup truck, but you should be perfectly safe here. I've got several guards posted on the property. The fence is electrified and the house is heavily armored. I can have more men and equipment brought out at the slightest hint of trouble."

"We'll be fine," said Rianna. "I know this place is a fortress. I helped plan the security, remember?"

Donald chuckled, but Sophie added motherly instructions. "I want you to relax, get some rest and remember to eat. You're a little too thin and you've got dark circles under your eyes."

Rianna grinned. "I have a good start on a tan, though."

"You'll have to tell me all about your adventure when we can visit longer," she said. "I know Donald's version is always heavily edited. It's nearly impossible to pry information out of him. He's the most close-mouthed man I've ever met."

Donald rose from the table, interrupting before she could get started on one of her favorite lectures. "Why don't the two of you get showered and settled a little before we leave," he suggested, deftly changing subjects. "I'll show Tremont around the house, introduce him to the agents and find him a change of clothes."

Rianna rose and stretched. She didn't have to be coaxed. She was feeling stuffed with Sophie's wonderful meal, and getting tired again. After excusing herself, she headed to her own room, stripped and climbed in the shower. A fresh Band-Aid protected her stitches while she allowed the water to pelt her with cleansing strength.

By the time she was dressed again, she felt squeaky clean for the first time in months. The soft, yellow cotton nightgown was nearly transparent, but comfortable. It fell to her knees and clung to her damp body. The matching robe buttoned up the front and wasn't much heavier, but she decided it added a respectable layer of clothing.

Within half an hour, she rejoined the others in the

living room. She gave goodbye hugs to Donald and Sophie, saw them to the door, and then watched as they pulled out of the driveway.

"Wonder why Sullivan was in such a hurry to leave?" Kyle reset the security system and followed her back to the living room. "I would have thought it'd be safer to wait until daylight."

"He's pretty fanatic about not letting Sophie get involved in agency business. I'm guessing she promised him she'd leave as soon as she knew I was okay."

"Has he ever used this place for a safe house before?"

"Never. He's always been adamant about security, but also about keeping this little family hideaway private. I'm sorry he's compromising the location now, but I'm sure glad to be here."

"They seem devoted to you."

"They're the best. I don't know what I would have done without them when my folks were killed. They could never legally adopt me since I'd been declared dead, so they had to create a whole new identity for me. They gave me their name along with their unconditional love and support."

"Not to mention risking his career if anyone learned what he'd done."

"That, too," she said.

Kyle moved to the fireplace and leaned an arm across the mantel. "Have you spent a lot of time here with them?"

Rianna perched on the arm of the sofa, near him, yet not touching. "Donald calls it our 'summer place,' but we sometimes spent the holidays here, too."

"They don't have any children of their own?"

"No, Sophie says they were always too wrapped up

in their careers to take the time. She's a university professor and they had decided against having children, until I got dumped on their doorstep. I was a confused, traumatized teenager, so it took more than the usual parenting skills to straighten me out. They're pretty special people.''

''They obviously love you.''

Rianna nodded, but wasn't sure she wanted to discuss that particular emotion. ''I can't believe you were jealous.'' She dared to tease, grinning at him. ''Did you really think I'd have one lover deliver me into the arms of another?''

Kyle held her gaze. ''I wasn't thinking with my head,'' he admitted, giving her a look so hot that it seared her.

She wanted to know if he'd been thinking with his heart or his hormones, but she didn't have the courage to ask. Instead, she rose and moved closer to him. He'd showered, shaved and dressed in a borrowed white T-shirt and black sweatpants.

Donald had never looked so good in either.

The shirt molded to Kyle's well-toned chest and hugged his lean, ridged stomach. The pants hung low on his hips, tightening over his strong, muscled thighs. Just the sight of him excited her, making her body tingle with anticipation.

As she drew closer, his arm snaked out and wrapped around her waist, drawing her against him. She flattened her hands on his chest, and then flexed her fingers, kneading him as a cat would do through the thin cloth.

''I'm starving for a kiss,'' he drawled, his gaze meeting with hers as his head slowly lowered. ''Everybody's been getting them except me.'' His tongue flicked out, bathing her lips with warmth and eliciting mewing encouragement from Rianna.

"Poor guy," she murmured, her breath mingling with his. He smelled of rich, dark coffee. "I'll have to see what I can do about that."

Next he nibbled at the corner of her mouth, and she slid her arms around his waist, rocking closer. Then his tongue bridged the barrier of her teeth. She moaned, leaning into his strength as her tongue slid against the hot length of his.

He plundered her mouth, making her weak with need. She felt the evidence of his arousal against her stomach and arched into its hard strength. Kyle made a husky noise of approval, so she continued to rub against him with rhythmic, coaxing pressure.

He raked his hands through her hair, clutching her head and tilting her mouth to fit more tightly against his own. Then he kissed her with steadily escalating passion. Deep, wet, drugging kisses that made her bones melt and her body turn liquid with desire. Primitive hunger erupted between them, so hot and fierce that they had to break apart to level some control.

"Damn, all I have to do is kiss you, and I start spiraling out of control," Kyle grumbled against her mouth, his breath coming in harsh pants.

"No complaints from me," she whispered, licking his lips with the tip of her tongue.

He closed his eyes and rested his forehead against hers. "I want to take my time with you tonight."

"I thought we did that last night."

"No," he argued. "You had your way with me last night. Tonight, I plan to have my way with you."

"Mmm...sounds fascinating," she said, bringing her hands up to cup his face. Their gazes locked, and she thrilled at the desire swirling in his eyes. "Couldn't we do both?"

"Both what?"

He seemed momentarily distracted by the curve of her cheek, planting a row of kisses along her jaw until she captured his wandering lips with her own. She couldn't get enough of him. She'd thought the need would abate once they'd become lovers, but it just kept sharpening.

"Couldn't we have it both ways?" she murmured against his mouth. "Hard and fast, then slow and easy?"

Her bold query had Kyle groaning and clutching her tighter. "Careful, beautiful, or you'll throw a monkey wrench into my well thought-out plans," he accused.

Rianna kissed him until they were both breathing faster. Kyle's hands convulsively stroked her back, and then slid to her hips. He grasped her buttocks, gathering handfuls of her gown and pulling her closer.

When they drew apart to gasp for air, he speared her with a dark, turbulent gaze. "Are you wearing anything under this gown?"

"Not a thing," she confessed, clinging to his shoulders. Her breasts were achy, so she rubbed them against his chest while arching her hips against his groin.

Kyle's big hands slid to her thighs, and he lifted her. Rianna wrapped her legs around his waist, straining for closer contact with the part of him that would make them one again.

"Easy." His command was rough with desire. He rocked his hips against the cradle of her body, and then swallowed her moan of pleasure.

Rianna gasped at the exquisite pleasure of being so close to him, his strength and heat. She took his tongue deeply into her mouth and continued to rub herself against him. He was carrying her to her room, but she didn't want to wait. She wanted him right now.

"Hard and fast," she said on her next gasp of air.

"Slow and easy." His mouth found the pulse at her neck. He sucked deeply, making her blood run even hotter.

"I can't stand it," she whimpered, arching her head back as his kisses poured over her neck and chest.

Kyle didn't respond. His mouth was too busy burrowing under the neckline of her robe and gown, suckling and seeking like a baby. Rianna brought one hand to her robe and started unfastening buttons. She wanted his mouth on her breasts.

"Stop," he insisted gruffly. They'd made it to her room where she'd left the bedside lamp burning. Kyle kicked the door shut, and then slowly lowered her to the bed.

She tried to pull him over her, but he resisted.

"I'll take care of these," he said, reaching for the tiny pearl buttons. Then, one by one, he slid them out of the holes.

Rianna decided that there was no sense trying to hurry him. She went still except for the heaving of her chest, and watched, fascinated, as he slowly undid her robe. He pushed the sides open and then watched as her breasts swelled against the thin fabric of the gown.

Her breathing grew more ragged as his eyes dilated with hot desire. Her nipples tightened wantonly, and a low groan rumbled from his chest. He reached out to cup both breasts in his hands, using his thumbs to stimulate them even more. Rianna cried out as tension coiled from her breasts to her womb.

When he leaned down to take a nipple into his

mouth, she arched against him in demand. His caress dampened the thin fabric and heightened her pleasure. Then he grew impatient with the barrier and slowly stripped off her robe and gown. His eyes gleamed with satisfaction when she lay naked before him. The brush of his gaze over her body made her flesh tingle and her pulse race even more.

Rianna reached out and beckoned him back into her arms. He leaned over her, but wouldn't be hurried. Taking one nipple into his mouth, he lapped it with his tongue while fondling the other breast with his palm.

She sunk her fingers into the thickness of his hair and held him close as pleasure coursed through her body. Impatient, she began to writhe against him and coax him with hungry little sounds that expressed her growing need.

"Slow and easy," he mumbled, sliding down her body to press wet kisses across her ribs, then her stomach.

Rianna clung to his hair, her body growing increasingly tense as his caresses dipped lower. Then he was sliding back over her and taking her mouth with a new surge of passion. She held his face in her hands while they shared more long, breathless kisses.

Kyle continued to stroke his hands down her sides to her legs. When one hand strayed to the apex of her thighs, she gasped and stiffened. He drew back slightly and gazed into her eyes.

"Let me love you," he begged huskily.

Rianna could barely nod, but when he touched her again, she felt the caress from head to toe. She began to tremble.

"Kyle!" Her cry was an urgent plea of surprised

need. His fingers were hard and hot, probing sensitive flesh no man had ever touched.

''Feel good?'' he whispered, locking gazes with her and demanding a response.

Feeling raw and exposed, she closed her eyes to keep him from seeing the vulnerability, but she nodded.

Then his mouth fell to her breast again. The combined caresses had her quivering so badly that she craved release. When his loving pushed her higher, she reached out frantically to strip off his shirt. She wanted him as naked and needy as she.

Chapter 11

Kyle halted the sensual assault long enough to move off the bed, quickly shed his clothes and grab a condom. Rianna opened her eyes and watched him bare his broad chest, then his lower body, exposing a jutting arousal that made her gasp.

She reached for him, but he grabbed her hands and pressed them to the bed on either side of her head. He stole another long kiss and began his loving all over again. All she could do was clutch his head as he alternately licked each of her nipples.

A tremor shot through her when he kissed her stomach, and then he was sliding lower in the bed, moving his hot kisses to even more sensitive areas. At the first touch of his mouth, she cried out again, arching her hips off the bed and pressing herself against his face.

Kyle grasped her thighs and held her close while he slowly explored her most sensitive flesh. The intimacy of his caresses stole her breath and shot fire through her body. A tremor shook her, followed by another and then another, coming harder and faster than she could draw in air and prepare for them.

She cried his name, her fingers digging into his hair in an attempt to stop the onslaught. She wanted him over her and in her, but he would not be hurried. When the climax finally hit her, she screamed his name in a long, low wail as heated pleasure swept her body.

Then it was all she could do to draw in a breath. Her lungs were on fire, her chest rising and falling with the effort to drag in air. Her toes were tightly curled and the rest of her body depleted. She felt limp and washed out, but still Kyle didn't stop his ardent loving.

He began kissing his way back up her body, over her quivering stomach, to each of her breasts, to her throat and finally to her mouth. When he'd moved above her again, she latched on to him, wrapping her arms tightly around his neck and holding him close as she silently, but passionately, thanked him for his loving with hard kisses.

She felt his arousal pressing against her hip and savored a renewed rush of desire. Sliding her hands down his body, she cupped his buttocks in her hands and massaged the tight flesh until he was moaning into her mouth. Then she wiggled beneath him until their bodies were once again aligned.

She could feel him pressing against her and shifted her legs wider to accommodate him. Then she pulled in a breath as he completed the union with one strong, sure stroke. Her body came alive with excitement and renewed desire.

Rianna shifted slightly to accept him more fully, then cupped his face in her hands. She stroked his cheeks, her gaze adoring. They stared into each other's eyes as he began the slow, steady dance of love in an ancient rhythm that would bring them ultimate satisfaction.

Soon they were scaling the heights together, each lost in the other as they shuddered to a climax that went beyond physical satisfaction to something much more intense and soul rending. Their hoarse cries of completion echoed in the silence of the room as Kyle's full weight collapsed on her.

Even though Rianna was struggling for each puff of air, she welcomed his weight, wrapping her arms tightly around him and holding him close. She relished the aftermath of their loving as their chests heaved, their bodies still intimately entangled.

In another minute, Kyle took his weight on his forearms and lifted his chest from hers, allowing them both a little freer breathing. He looked into her eyes again, delving into her soul. She wasn't sure what he hoped to see there.

I could fall desperately in love with you!

The words reverberated in her head, but she didn't say them out loud. The thought was still too new and too incredibly frightening. She perversely wanted Kyle to say the words to her, yet feared saying them to him. She waited, wondering if he expected her to proclaim her feelings.

When they could breathe again, she finally broke the silence with a gentle taunt. ''If that was slow and easy, why am I sweating?''

His husky male laughter filled the room. Rolling onto his side, he pulled her across his chest. Then he smoothed her damp hair behind her ears, continuing to study her features with his warm gaze.

''You're incredible,'' he insisted, his voice thick. ''And you make me feel incredible. Sweat and all.''

"You're the one who's incredible," she teased, stroking his face with gentle fingers. "All I did was enjoy."

Laughter rumbled from his chest again, and she loved the feel of it against her breasts.

"Glad to be of service, ma'am," he replied, brushing a soft kiss across her lips, then pulling her head down to his shoulder. "I didn't mean to exhaust you. I planned to do all the work, but I got a little carried away."

"Okay by me," she mumbled against his damp skin.

"You've had a rough few days, and I haven't been letting you recuperate. Didn't that ER doctor advise against too much strenuous exercise?"

"Hmm…" Rianna practically purred as she snuggled against him. "What's he know? I've never felt better in my life."

She felt the flexing of his chest muscles again, and delighted in the fact that she'd made him feel good, too. Heaven help her, but she was in way over her head. She loved everything about him.

"Are we going to sleep?" he asked once they'd both quieted.

"We're just resting our eyes," she mumbled, her whole body limp and lethargic. She couldn't even lift her lashes.

"Does that mean we can make love again in a little while?" he teased, nibbling on her ear.

"Sure." The word was slurred.

He continued to stroke her hair with one hand while caressing her back with the other. "Good, 'cause I really like making love to you."

Rianna heard him, but couldn't find the strength to

respond. She drifted to sleep, feeling more safe and contented than she could ever remember.

He woke her near dawn, his hands and mouth at her breasts, his teeth and tongue plucking at her nipples. Desire flowed through her like lava, thick and aflame, stirring her senses to a red-hot frenzy of need. He drove her to new heights before they sated themselves once again. Depleted, they fell into a deep, passion-drugged sleep.

The sun had neared its zenith by the time Rianna woke again. Kyle had rolled to one side of the bed. She watched him sleep for a long time, just savoring the sight of him. She felt tempted to wake him the way he'd done her, but decided he needed the rest. He'd had a busy night, and she had to go to the bathroom.

He was still sleeping soundly after she'd showered. She pulled on an old, faded blue T-shirt and matching gym shorts before leaving her room and heading for the kitchen. After making a pot of coffee, she waited for it to perk, and then carried a cupful into the living room.

The room was bathed in sunlight. She pulled back the drapes and opened the window a crack. It had rained sometime during the night, making the air clean and clear. Inhaling deeply, she took a minute to watch the birds at Sophie's feeder and enjoy the uncomplicated normalcy.

Everything seemed quiet, but Rianna knew there was nothing uncomplicated or normal about her life, however much she'd like to wish for it. She needed to talk to Donald and see what was happening in D.C.

Perching on the edge of the sofa, she picked up the

phone and dialed his number. He picked up after the second ring.

"Good morning, Mr. Deputy Director," she teased him, using her private nickname.

"Good morning, Special Agent," he teased back.

Rianna smiled. "Everything all right with you and Sophie?"

"Just fine. She nagged me all the way to the apartment last night, but I stayed tough. I refused to turn around and head back to the cabin, even though she came up with some pretty good reasons why we should."

"She's a woman of many skills."

"You can say that again. After nearly twenty years of marriage, she's pretty adept at using them on me."

"And you love it."

"Damn right."

The deep satisfaction in his voice widened her smile.

"You sound pretty chipper this morning," said Donald. "Get a good night's sleep?"

Rianna was glad he couldn't see the blush that warmed her cheeks. She tried to keep her tone casual. "It was great to be home in my own bed."

"I imagine it was. Kyle up and about yet?"

"He's not up yet, but I just brewed coffee, so the smell will probably lure him out soon."

"I hate to dampen your mood, but I'm afraid I have some disturbing news for him."

Rianna hated it, too, more than he could know. She didn't want the ugliness of law enforcement intruding on her world today. Her heart grew heavy at the thought of Kyle becoming more deeply enmeshed in her problems.

Anytime she dared to take a risk on happiness, something always happened to burst her bubble and threaten those she loved. Hands shaking, she set the cup down in the saucer and tried to mentally prepare herself for the worst.

"What's wrong?"

"Haroldson's lawyer is trying to convince a judge that he's a law-abiding citizen who's been victimized by a con artist. He's claiming Kyle kidnapped you and assaulted his employees."

She swallowed hard, but kept her tone calm. "Is he threatening to file counter charges?"

"I told the assistant U.S. attorney that you'd gone with him of your own free will. I doubt his lawyers will press it any further."

Rianna's chest grew tighter. Kyle could face charges, however flimsy, for coming to her aid. To a man with his deep respect for the law, it would be the ultimate insult. His reputation was being sullied, yet there was nothing he could do. He didn't deserve the grief or the injustice after years of service to his country.

Rianna's feelings of guilt just kept escalating. "I don't want him to face charges because of me."

"Shouldn't be a problem, it's just an unexpected glitch and some extra red tape."

"Gregory is famous for causing glitches," she growled. "I'll tell Kyle you're working to get it straightened out."

"There's more." Donald prefaced his next announcement with a gentle tone he reserved for really bad news.

She tensed, her fingers fisting. "What else?"

"I figured Haroldson's mole in the agency identified Tremont, so I sent some agents to keep an eye on his house. We guessed Haroldson would do the same once he knew the two of you were traveling together.''

Nausea rose in her throat. Why hadn't she considered that angle? Gregory always sought retribution against anyone who crossed him.

She remembered the pride in Kyle's voice when he'd described his home and dreaded hearing the details. ''I'm not going to like it, am I.''

'''Fraid not,'' Donald said on a sigh. ''The agents did a check on his place just in time to keep it from going up in flames. Someone had trashed the house and set the shop on fire. Most of his workshop was destroyed. The house had some smoke damage, but it's still structurally sound and can be remodeled. I've already hired a team to clean and do the interior work.''

Rianna closed her eyes and sank back against the sofa cushions. Her stomach churned, her thoughts filled with anger and shame. Kyle's grandfather's shop had been destroyed, and it was all her fault.

If he hadn't helped her, he wouldn't be involved with the kind of conscienceless people who wreaked havoc for a living. He'd chosen to leave that world, but he'd been tossed back into it on her account. She hated being the cause of so much destruction. She was a jinx to anyone who dared get too close.

''Mary?'' Donald interrupted her black thoughts.

''I'm still here. It makes me sick,'' she said, giving a sad sigh. Then her tone grew stronger and took on a low snarl. ''I want him to pay, Donald. He has so much death and destruction to pay for.''

''He's going to pay dearly,'' he swore. ''We're making sure of that. I can't imagine anything worse for a fastidious control freak that being incarcerated for life. The AUSA will petition for the death penalty, but a lifetime in prison will be Haroldson's ultimate punishment."

Rianna supposed he was right. She just wanted guarantees, but she knew there were none.

"I think I hear Kyle in the shower now. As soon as he comes out, I'll tell him what's been happening. I just hate it that he's not free to go home and take care of everything himself."

"Hopefully soon. I'm staying in the city today to try to stay abreast of things."

"Thanks." She tried to sound more upbeat, not wanting to add to his worries. "Give Sophie a hug for me."

"You bet."

Rianna held the phone to her ear for a while after she heard the click of his disconnection and the hum of the dial tone. Then she slowly lowered the receiver back to its base. Her thoughts were whirling and none of them were pleasant.

She'd caused Kyle nothing but trouble, yet she was helpless to halt the chain of events at this point. There had to be a way to make things right. She'd think of something, and soon.

Her legs were a little unsteady when she rose from the sofa, but she mentally scolded herself. She didn't like feeling weak and fearful at the thought of Gregory going after Kyle. The emotional involvement scared her even more than did the threat of violence. She could handle his vengeance if it was directed at her, but not at those she loved.

Kyle joined her shortly after she started cooking breakfast. Freshly shaved and showered, he set her pulse skittering. He looked rested, yet predatory, like a contented, sexy tiger on the prowl. The gleam in his eyes sent heat through her veins.

His hair, on head and chest, glistened with moisture, coiling into tight curls and tempting her to touch. All he wore was a pair of Donald's too-large jeans, with the waist sliding low on his hips. She had a hunch he wasn't wearing anything under them, and that thought made her tingle with anticipation.

He greeted her with a kiss that sent her senses swirling and temporarily blocked all thought from her mind. He tasted of mint and hungry man. She clung to him, savoring his solid warmth and uninhibited loving.

"Good morning," she finally whispered against his lips.

"It's okay now," he told her as he nibbled at her mouth. "But it wasn't so good when I woke up in a cold, empty bed."

Rianna laughed softly. "That is terrible," she teased, running her hands over his shoulders, loving the satin-smooth feel of his skin. "I couldn't stay. Nature called, so I decided I might as well get up and find us something to eat."

Kyle's stomach chose to growl at that very minute, making them both laugh. By mutual agreement, they dished up the scrambled eggs she'd cooked and made some toast. Rianna poured them both some juice, then sat across from him at the table.

They ate in silence because she didn't want to discuss what was on her mind. Kyle gave her a few searching looks, but she couldn't think of anything cheery and casual to say. She wasn't in the mood for small talk. She was busy trying to find a way to tell him what she'd learned this morning.

When they'd finished, Kyle carried their dishes to

the sink and ran some water over them. He poured them each a cup of coffee. Rianna watched his every movement while shredding her paper napkin in nervousness. Her legendary control seemed nonexistent when it came to this man.

She thanked him when he placed the cup in front of her, sipped at her coffee, and stalled for more time.

"Looks like a nice day," he finally said, breaking the silence. "Sullivan said there's a stream out back where we can do some fishing."

She nodded and glanced toward the window. Sunlight streamed through the pane, bathing the room with early afternoon light. She, too, had thought the day perfect, until she'd called Donald.

"It does look like a perfect summer day. I know where he keeps his fishing tackle. Maybe we can catch tonight's dinner."

"Fishing sounds good. What else is on the agenda?"

"Nothing much, I guess. I want to watch the video Donald confiscated from Gregory's estate."

"We'll do that first," he said, taking a long swallow of coffee. Rianna watched his throat work, and hers grew tight.

When he set down the cup, he reached out and grasped her hand. She gave him a wary glance, but didn't resist when he tugged harder. Rising from her chair, she moved close enough for him to wrap his hands around her waist. Then he lifted her until she straddled his lap.

Her bare legs slid over his jeans-covered thighs, the friction sending a sizzle of sensation over her sensitized skin. She splayed her hands on his chest and felt more heat coursing through her.

"Wanna tell me what's worrying you so much this morning?" he asked gently, his gaze locking with hers.

Rianna dropped her lashes. Emotion clogged her throat, making her reluctant to speak in case she embarrassed herself.

Kyle lifted her chin, stared into her eyes. His voice went low and intimate. "You're not upset about last night, are you? Did I move too fast? Do something that made you uncomfortable? Cross some invisible boundary?"

"No!" She cupped his face in her hands, wanting him to know that her mood had nothing to do with the physical side of their relationship. "Absolutely not. I loved every touch and kiss and caress. I swear it on my life. Last night was incredible," she whispered softly.

Some of the tension drained from his features. Before he could comment, Rianna pressed her lips to his. She slid her tongue into his mouth, trying to communicate without words. Trying to show him the emotion she couldn't describe.

The kiss was long and deep and sweet. Kyle's hands slid down her body, pulling her closer. She wrapped her arms around his neck, savoring the taste and feel of him. One kiss led to another and another.

Then guilt had her pulling back. She couldn't keep stalling or pretending everything was all right. He might not even want to touch her when he learned the whole truth. A tremor shook her at the dark thought.

He drew in a deep breath and then sighed heavily. His hands tightened at her hips, fingers massaging.

"Why don't you tell me what's bothering you?"

She dropped her gaze again. "I talked to Donald this

morning. He had some bad news and some worse news.''

She felt Kyle stiffen. He lifted her chin again and forced her to look at him. His eyes darkened stormily.

''Haroldson's been freed on bond?'' he asked tightly.

''No!'' Rianna shook her head vigorously. ''At least, not yet, but his attorney is trying to sway a judge.''

''That's no surprise.'' Kyle visibly relaxed. ''Then, what's the latest development? Let's start with the bad news.''

She stroked his face, smoothing his brows, the strong line of his jaw and the curve of his cheek. She loved touching him, and showed it in the tenderness of her caresses.

''Gregory's trying to make you out to be the bad guy.''

Kyle's eyes narrowed. After a brief hesitation, he said, ''We already assumed that. What's different?''

''He's claiming you assaulted his staff and threatening to file charges. Donald's sure they won't stick, but you should stay put until he gets things straightened out.''

He seemed to relax a little more. ''That's not so bad,'' he teased, sliding his hands to the small of her back and rubbing her through the soft fabric. ''I like the idea of staying holed up with you for days or maybe even weeks.''

Rianna didn't share his smile. ''That's not the worst of it,'' she warned.

''So, what's the worst?''

''Gregory had some men vandalize your house. They destroyed a lot of your personal possessions and set it on fire.'' Rianna paused, swallowing the tears clogging her throat. "The house can be repaired, but your wood-shop burned to the ground."

Kyle went rigid. For a second, he looked so fierce and angry that her breathing faltered. She would have slid off his lap, but his hands tightened at her hips. She wouldn't blame him if he hated her and rued the day he'd met her, yet the thought of him harboring such feelings brought more tears to her eyes.

"I'm so sorry," she whispered, hating her own shaky voice and emotional upheaval. "I'm so sorry that helping me means losing everything you've worked for, for so long."

"Don't!" he commanded, his voice rough. "Don't start blaming yourself for something totally out of your control."

"I can't help it," she whispered, tears welling in her eyes. She blinked rapidly. "You shouldn't be punished for doing what's right. It just isn't fair."

"It'll be okay," he insisted, visibly forcing himself to relax. "Everything's insured. I don't own anything that can't be replaced. Nothing."

"What about the things that belong to your customers or your grandfather? You said you refinish valuable antiques."

"I cleared all that stuff out of the shop before I left. The rest is just…stuff. Nothing special. Just things."

She gave him a dubious stare.

His features reflected a myriad of emotions, and then his expression went blank. She could tell that he'd deliberately blocked his own feelings to soothe hers. When she continued to stare at him in silence, he rationalized.

"In fact, Haroldson might have done me a favor. I

have replacement insurance. I can get all those old, secondhand tools replaced with brand-new ones.''

His attempt to make her feel better brought another rush of tears to her eyes. Try as she might, she couldn't keep a couple from spilling down her cheek.

Kyle groaned in protest, then flicked out his tongue to capture a teardrop. ''Don't,'' he mumbled against her skin, licking and kissing his way down her cheek. ''Don't cry. I can't stand it. All the bad news isn't worth one of your tears.''

Rianna smothered a soft sob against his mouth. He returned her kiss gently at first, but she didn't want gentle. Badly needing reassurance, she kissed him with a force and hunger that quickly wiped everything but him from her mind. He pulled her tighter against his chest while they devoured each other with lips and tongues and teeth.

She strained to get closer, pressing her breasts against the solid wall of his chest and tightening her grip on his neck. Her thighs clenched around his and their bodies rocked against each other in rhythmic demand.

When they finally drew apart long enough to catch their breath, Kyle nuzzled her neck. He pressed hot kisses on the pulse frantically beating there.

Rianna sighed, wondering at his ability to make her forget everything but the taste and feel of his body. Then the guilt crept back into her thoughts.

''I still wish there was something I could do to make it better,'' she murmured against his cheek.

He deliberately misinterpreted her words. ''There is something,'' he suggested, his breath warm on her ear.

''What?''

''You could take off your shirt.''

Surprised, Rianna leaned back in his arms and stared at him. The gleam in his eyes was totally wicked and just as totally irresistible. It offered not only acceptance, but also the promise of the same sweet satisfaction she always found in his arms. The thought dried her tears, but she smacked him on the arm.

"You're so bad."

"Because you're so good."

Her laugh held a note of surprise, and warmth invaded her cheeks. He was bold and audacious and so impossibly sexy. She wanted to be bold and sexy, but didn't know how to go about it. Then Kyle took hold of her shirttail and slowly pulled it over her head.

She hadn't bothered with a bra.

The sudden darkening of his eyes as he stared at her made her breasts ache for attention.

"So beautiful," he murmured.

She felt the damp heat of his breath an instant before he took her into his mouth. A shiver raced over her as fire spiked from breast to womb. Her muscles clenched in passionate anticipation.

Burying her fingers in his hair, Rianna arched her back to give him better access. His body responded, his arousal swelling and pressing against her.

"There's another way you can make it up to me," he said, while shifting his mouth from one breast to the other.

"How's that?"

"Unsnap these damn jeans."

Rianna laughed softly, thrilled by his impatience and eager to do his bidding. In a matter of minutes, he'd coerced her from guilt ridden to highly aroused. Being with Kyle offered a roller coaster of emotions—one that she wanted to ride as long as possible.

* * *

Once they'd sated each other, they took a long, leisurely shower together. They didn't make love again, but they explored each other with an intimate thoroughness that kept their bodies singing with sexual tension.

After dressing, they spent what was left of the afternoon wandering around the grounds. They rechecked the security system and touched base with the agents posted at the front entrance and back property line.

The protection team worked eight-hour shifts, changing at eight a.m., four p.m. and midnight. Rianna didn't know them, but she recognized a couple of names. She asked that her personal thanks be passed on to all the team members.

By early evening, they were ready to eat again, and finished off the leftover pot roast and pie. Then they settled in the living room to watch the eighteen-year-old video Donald had confiscated from the Haroldson estate.

Her family had been caught in the camera's eye at intervals during one of Gregory's early staff parties. First they'd been gathered around the buffet table, then their own table and finally near the dance floor.

Rianna wept quietly as the film progressed.

She'd been about ten at the time, with pigtails, missing front teeth, and a frilly party dress. Jimmy had worn new clothes, too, but she remembered him complaining about them being tight and uncomfortable. He'd been so small that he'd begged their dad to lift him so he could see everything.

Her mother looked wonderfully alive and heartbreakingly dear in those years before the lines of strain marked her lovely skin. Her father had been so young and handsome and confident, his features free of the constant worry she'd seen in the years after he'd left Gregory's employ.

For just an instant in time, Rianna had them back again and felt whole. Even though the video was of poor quality, she'd treasure it always. It held a rare glimpse of her family when they'd still been normal and happy.

Her heart ached for the decent people she knew them to be and the price they'd paid for their integrity. It pleased her to know she'd brought Gregory a few steps closer to justice. She silently renewed her vow to see him punished.

"You look like your mother," said Kyle, gathering her in his arms and offering comfort, "but you have your dad's nose and you're built more like him."

"Thank you," she said, sniffling but making an effort to control the flow of tears.

Her mother had always cursed her short, round body, while her dad had been on the thin side. Rianna loved knowing she carried physical traits from each of them.

She paused the tape, rewound it, and then hit replay. Kyle never complained, watching the same few minutes of film over and over again.

His sensitivity and compassion touched her more deeply than she'd have thought possible. He just kept giving of himself, and she kept taking. She was so incredibly needy. Their relationship seemed too one-sided to be healthy, but she tried not to dwell on the negative.

When Rianna finally found the strength to shut off the VCR, she turned into Kyle's arms and pressed her mouth to his, trying to convey all the complexity of her feelings in one long, lingering kiss.

He responded, as always, with a need that matched hers. She wanted the sight and scent and feel of him indelibly printed in her memories, so she relished every touch and kiss.

Kyle accepted the intensity of her loving and responded in kind, equally intent on making memories.

Chapter 12

Later, they cuddled in front of the TV, fed each other popcorn and watched a romantic comedy. Kyle said it gave him naughty ideas. Rianna laughed and agreed that they'd have to experiment a little, but maybe tomorrow.

"Are you telling me you don't want to make love again tonight?" he teased.

"Are you telling me you do?" she asked.

He took his time responding. "The spirit's willing but the flesh is weak," he explained, grinning.

The expression on his face made her laugh harder. "There's nothing weak about your flesh," she chided, knowing he was more worried about her being tender. "I'm willing to vouch for the strength of your body parts any time you like."

That brought back the wicked grin she loved so much.

"I'll remember that."

When they finally went to bed, they held each other close, mingling soft whispers with even softer kisses and caresses. It was another unique and wonderful experience for Rianna. One she knew she'd treasure the rest of her life.

They fell asleep in each other's arms, but her dreams were anything but peaceful. She dreamed of a house on fire, a raging inferno with black, billowing smoke and out-of-control flames licking at a midnight sky. Silent screams tore at her throat as she watched, terrified and helpless, while her family's home burned.

The dream had plagued her in the early years after she'd been orphaned, but now it took on a new and sinister twist. As she watched the house burning, she saw Kyle's face at a window. He stared at her, his expression accusing and filled with hate as the flames engulfed him.

Rianna fought her way out of the nightmare. Tremors shook her body until she could force the terror of her dream out of her mind. Soaked in sweat but chilled to the bone, she felt locked in a time warp. Forcing herself to breathe deeply, she tried to rationalize the horror her mind had conjured, but it didn't help.

Then Kyle's arms enfolded her, drawing her close to his side. He sensed her trauma and mumbled soft, reassuring words of comfort. His hands gently stroked her back and shoulders until some of the tension began to subside.

She finally relaxed, snuggling closer and basking in his tenderness. Her renegade was so incredibly special. She loved him beyond words and reason. She wanted to block out all the ugliness and take comfort in his arms, but she knew she wouldn't get another minute's rest.

When he'd drifted back to sleep, she stayed in his arms until his grip relaxed. Then she carefully slid from his side and climbed out of bed. Dawn was nearing, so she knew it wouldn't be too early to call Donald. She tiptoed into the living room and phoned his apartment.

He answered and they exchanged greetings, but he immediately sensed her tension. "What's wrong?"

"I think it's time for us to get Kyle out of this situation," she told him, her tone clipped and decisive.

There was a pause, and then Donald's response. "I agree, but I got the impression there's something special going on between the two of you."

"There is, but there's no way we can pursue it right now. Kyle's already given up too much. He deserves to have his life back," she insisted. "Have charges been filed against him?"

"No. I took care of it. The AUSA told Haroldson's lawyers the charges wouldn't stick."

"Then there's no reason Kyle can't go home."

"It's for the best. You don't need any distractions right now."

The thought of him leaving made her heart ache, so she suggested a way to make it easier. "I'm not going to give him a choice."

"Maybe you'd better tell me exactly what you are planning."

She could almost hear his frown, but that didn't deter her. "I'm going to be the one who leaves. I'll go on up the coast a ways." Rianna didn't mention her destination over the phone, but Donald would know.

Margaret Wilding had been her foster mother for a short time before the Sullivans had taken her in. Margaret had no blood relatives, but she was a surrogate aunt to many. Her house had always been considered an alternative safe house, since she had no traceable connection to anyone in the agency.

"You're going to drive my car?"

"If you don't mind."

"No problem. Take Special Agent Payne with you. He's young and won't mind being gone a few days. He's also smart and totally trustworthy. I'll let him know about the change of plans."

Now that the decision had his stamp of approval, she felt all sad and weepy again. She wouldn't cry. She was supposed to be a professional and this was a professional decision.

Clearing her throat, she said, "Thanks, Donald. I can't tell you how much it means to me."

"You just take care of yourself and call when you're settled. Don't take any chances, and don't worry about Tremont. I'll deal with him when he calls to raise hell."

"I'm sorry to dump it on you, but I'd rather leave without him knowing. He'll try to talk me out of it and make things even more complicated."

She didn't want to waste time arguing with Kyle. It would be hard enough to leave him. He'd be hurt, angry and probably hate her for taking matters into her own hands, but she could live with that as long as she knew he was safe. He needed time to rebuild his home and his life.

"Leave him a note so he doesn't freak out when he realizes you're gone. I'll explain when I get there."

"He'll be furious."

They both knew that was a gross understatement.

"Yeah. Can't say I blame him, but I've been a casualty of his wrath before and survived. It's part of the job description."

Rianna thanked him again, and then hung up the phone. The weight of her decision lay heavily on her heart, but she knew it was the right thing to do. It was the only solution at this point.

He'd be so disappointed in her, and that saddened her most of all. She'd lose his trust and respect, but he'd be free of the baggage she brought to the relationship. She didn't want him embroiled in months, possibly years, of legal battles to bring Gregory and his men to justice.

She wanted him to have a choice. It was the only thing she could give him, and it was important to her own emotional well-being. She couldn't live in fear of losing him the way she'd lost her family.

After quietly packing a suitcase, she took one precious minute to study his sleeping form. Her heart ached as she slipped out of the house into the darkness.

Kyle woke when sunshine poured into the bedroom. He slowly opened his eyes and blinked at the invading light, dragging himself from the deepest sleep he'd had in months. He stretched, enjoying the pull of his muscles as he worked out the stiffness.

His morning arousal throbbed into life, garnering his full attention. A deep, anticipatory smile creased his face and a deeper yearning settled into his gut at the thought of burying himself in the sweet, passionate woman at the side.

Then he reached for Rianna.

She wasn't in bed, which dampened his spirits considerably. He wanted a kiss and a snuggle and some special loving to start their day. He'd gotten really fond of having her in his arms.

Tossing back the sheet, he climbed from bed and

headed for the bathroom, hoping to find his ladylove close by. He didn't hear the shower running, but she could be naked and need some help getting dry. His smile returned at the thought.

But the bathroom was empty with no evidence that Rianna had recently showered. After brushing his teeth and splashing some water on his face he went back to the bedroom and pulled on a pair of gym shorts. Then he followed the smell of freshly brewed coffee to the kitchen, thinking she must be cooking some breakfast for them.

But the kitchen was empty, too, and the coffeepot had a timer. There was no beautiful woman waiting for him.

Suddenly, all the hair on his body stood on end. He tensed, his body going rigid as he realized how unnaturally quiet the place seemed. There was no sound indicating the presence of anyone else in the house.

"Rianna!"

Fear surged through him as he yelled and tore through the house searching for her.

"Rianna!"

How stupid could he be? He should have realized she wasn't here the instant he woke alone. He continued to yell her name as he did a room by room search, checking closets, the basement and attic until he grew hoarse and there was nowhere else to check.

Retracing his steps, he looked out windows, checking the grounds, trying to convince himself that she'd just slipped outside for a minute. He opened the kitchen door and yelled for her again.

She didn't answer, and the silence caused a new upheaval of panic. Had Haroldson's men gotten past the other agents? Could they have snatched her from the house without him knowing? How could he have been so stupid? He'd relaxed his guard too soon, too much, and had slept like the dead.

He'd failed her again, and his chest constricted at the thought of her being alone or at the mercy of Haroldson's goons. He had to find her.

"Rianna!"

Fear and pain mingled in the frantic repetition of her name. What if the agents outside were unconscious or dead? He reached for the phone, quickly punching in the beeper number for one of the guards. Then he held the receiver to his ear and waited for a response, hoping there would be one.

When the phone rang, he growled his relief at the caller. "This is Tremont. Where the hell is Agent Sullivan?"

The reply came hesitantly. "Would that be the deputy director you're looking for, sir, or Special Agent Sullivan?"

Kyle ground his teeth in frustration at the man's calm question. "Special Agent Sullivan. You're supposed to be guarding her, remember?"

"No, sir," the agent replied quietly. "Special Agent Sullivan left a couple of hours ago with Special Agent Payne."

"What do you mean, left?" he shouted, body shuddering as his temper shot upward. "Where the hell did they go? The grocery store? She's not supposed to leave the house without armed guards. Why the hell would they risk going anywhere?"

"That I don't know, sir. My orders are to stay here and make sure nobody gets close to the house. You'll have to call the deputy director if you want details."

Kyle swore viciously as he jammed the receiver

down and then lifted it again for a dial tone. He punched in Sullivan's private number, then waited the interminable time it took for the other man to answer.

"Sullivan."

He didn't waste time with pleasantries. "Where the hell is Rianna? I can't believe you let her leave this house. Have you lost your mind!" he exploded.

"You're always so cheerful in the morning, Tremont."

Sullivan's attempt at lightness didn't impress him. "Your man outside said she left with Payne. What the hell is going on?" he snapped.

"We decided it was time for her to move to another safe house."

"You *what?*" Kyle knew he was losing it. He was yelling at the top of his lungs because he could barely draw air into them. A suffocating tightness had settled there.

"You moved her without clearing it with me? You let her sneak out of here in the dead of night with one young, inexperienced agent? What the hell is wrong with you?"

"We decided it was best," Sullivan explained patiently.

Kyle heard the sympathy in his voice, and it chilled him to the bone. "Are you saying Rianna agreed without an argument or a word of goodbye?"

"She said she'd leave a note."

That didn't reassure him in the least. "I want to know where she went." His tone went cold and implacable.

"You know I can't tell you that."

"Can't?" Kyle's response was feral, but he knew he was wasting his time. He slammed down the phone and starting prowling the house again, looking for the note Rianna was supposed to have left him.

He found it on the telephone stand in the living room. A plain white envelope bearing his name was propped against a flower vase. Hand trembling, he reached for it and tore the envelope to get to the scrap of paper inside.

Dear Kyle,
I'm sorry to leave so abruptly, but it was time for me to move to another safe house.

Please go home and take care of your house and business. I promise I'll have Donald keep you apprised of the agency's case against Gregory.

Thank you so much for keeping me safe. I'll be forever grateful that you were the one who helped me escape and begin to heal.

Yours, Rianna

Yours, Rianna? Kyle raked a hand through his hair, shaking his head in rejection of that. She wasn't his and never had been, except maybe in his mind. If she really cared about him, why wasn't she here?

Why had she slipped away in secret to escape him? Had he gotten too close to her heart or had she just feared he was beginning to care more than she could ever reciprocate?

Gone. He couldn't believe she'd been coldhearted enough to leave with nothing more than a few pathetic words on a slip of paper, to leave knowing there was no way he could follow to her newest hiding place.

Impotent fury raged through him, followed by a pain so excruciating that he began to tremble. He couldn't move, couldn't seem to catch his breath.

Then a sound near the door snapped his head in that direction. He wasn't sure he could trust his eyes. Rianna had entered the house and slowly moved toward him. Her gaze settled on his face. Then she spoke quietly, hesitantly.

"I was hoping I could make it back before you woke up and found that," she said.

Her voice sounded as shaky as he felt. Kyle soaked up the sweetness of it, his eyes feasting on her. She looked so good, so precious, so sweetly repentant. His throat tightened and his body hardened. The violent, involuntary reactions had him grinding his teeth.

He crushed the note in his fist, then wadded it into a tight ball and threw it as hard as he could. It didn't go far, but the action offered minimal relief to the crippling tension of his body.

He turned and headed to the bedroom without a word. Once there, he stripped off his shorts, and pulled on jeans and a T-shirt. His movements were fast and furious, but no amount of activity could calm his seething anger—an anger directed at himself more than Rianna. He should know by now that caring too much always led to heartache and regrets.

He'd just sat on the bed to put on socks, when Rianna appeared in the doorway.

"You'd better keep your distance," he warned as he fought to control his temper. She'd wounded him with her rejection and mistrust. When he hurt, he got angry.

"I don't blame you for being furious—" she started.

"Don't you?" he snapped. "That's generous."

She flinched at his tone, but Kyle was beyond caring. She'd made it clear she wanted him out of her life as painlessly as possible. So be it. He'd leave and never look back. He didn't need the humiliation of being dumped. Didn't need the pain and anger and gnawing need.

"I wish you'd let me explain," she begged.

"Explain!" he shouted, surging to his feet and glaring at her. "Forget the explanations. Actions speak a whole helluva lot louder than words."

"I'm sorry—"

He cut her off with another sharp exclamation, too angry to listen to reason. "Save the sorries. You made your point, and you're right. It's time we parted ways."

"You're going?"

"That's right. I'm going home and wiping my hands of this whole mess."

She flinched and went pale. His chest tightened, and he cursed himself for caring, then funneled the emotion into more anger.

"I'm tired of being jerked around to suit your needs. I'm tired of playing puppet with you and Sullivan controlling the strings. I thought we had something special between us, but that must have been just another attempt to keep me in line so that you could jerk me around some more. Well, I'm not interested in explanations or apologies."

When he'd finished, they stared at each other for a pregnant moment. She waited to make sure he'd finished his tirade. Then she looked him straight in the eyes.

"I hadn't been gone an hour before I realized I had to come back." Her voice quivered, and she swallowed hard. When he didn't interrupt or start yelling again, she continued.

"I've never thought of myself as a coward, but leaving here without a word was a spineless way to handle the situation. I rationalized the decision in all the usual

ways, but the truth finally hit me. I was running away
again. The same way I've done most of my life, and
I'm tired of running.''

Her voice dropped to a shaky whisper. She shifted
her gaze so that she wasn't looking directly at him
anymore, but Kyle couldn't take his eyes off her. She
looked so fragile and weary, so unsure and unlike the
lover he knew.

He needed to stroke his anger and pretend he didn't
care, yet he couldn't bear seeing her so shaken.

''I got scared, really, truly scared, and I hate being
scared,'' she confessed raggedly.

When her lips quivered, his gut tightened. Her admission cracked through some of his newly polished
armor. A good part of his remaining anger stemmed
from the scare she'd given him, but they needed to hash
this out.

''I thought you were fearless,'' he taunted.

''I thought so, too,'' she said, searching his face with
eyes that made his skin prickle with awareness. ''After
my family was murdered, I couldn't shake the guilt of
surviving. No amount of counseling can completely
wipe that out of a person's system. Donald accused me
of having a death wish, and maybe he was right.''

''You have a death wish?'' The question seemed
ripped from his soul.

''Not anymore,'' she swore. ''That's what frightens
me so much. I didn't used to care if I lived or died. I
only cared about vengeance and seeing Gregory
brought to justice. Nothing and nobody ever tempted
me to veer from a path of self-destruction.''

Kyle finally realized what she was telling him. ''Until me,'' he injected gruffly.

''Until you,'' she answered softly, her gaze locking

again with his. "You made me care again. You made me start thinking of a future and the possibility of a real, normal life. You made me feel things I didn't want to feel. It…scares me."

Her honesty and vulnerability stole the rest of the anger from Kyle, leaving him just as vulnerable. He unclenched his fists and took the steps that brought her within reach. Then he cupped her head in his hands, tilting it upward and forcing her to lock gazes with him.

"Do you care? Really care about more than the great sex?" he asked, his thumbs stroking the softness of her cheeks.

"Yes," she whispered softly.

He closed his eyes, and then reopened them. He wasn't ready to proclaim his everlasting love, nor was he ready to let her go. "I think we've got something special going, and we should give it a chance."

Rianna's expression went from vulnerable to incredibly sad. "I don't see how," she insisted. "I've been on this crusade to punish Gregory for too long to let it go now. My life can never be my own. Even if he's found guilty and put behind bars, there will be years and years of appeals."

He could feel her pain and disillusionment as she continued to bare her heart.

"He'll still want me dead, and he'll still have the wealth and power to have me hunted. I'll never be completely safe, and I'd never ask anyone I care about to live that kind of life. I saw what it did to my parents. I couldn't bear having it happen all over again."

Kyle finally cut off the flow of words with a kiss. He hadn't planned to kiss her, but he didn't know any other way to stop the outpouring of worry and fear. He understood her concerns now, but they'd find a way.

"If we let him destroy our relationship, then he wins," he told her, nibbling on her lips. He felt her sharp intake of breath and knew she understood. "He's been controlling your life for too long," he added. "It stops here. You're not the only one who wants him to pay for his crimes. It's us against him."

With that, he dipped his head.

Rianna wrapped her arms around him and leaned into his kiss. Their mouths locked, tongues searching, soothing, and then demanding. In a matter of seconds, heat exploded between them, but she suddenly pulled away.

"There's something else."

Kyle knew by her tone and expression that he wasn't going to like it.

"I was wrong to run today, but I'm right about you going home. You need to take care of things in Texas, or Gregory will have succeeded in destroying that, too."

"The insurance company can handle the details," he argued, not voicing his own concerns.

"We need some distance between us for a while."

He wanted to argue, but she pressed a finger against his lips. "Please," she coaxed.

Kyle nodded, and she continued.

"The psychologists warned me about becoming too dependent on anyone who helped me escape the undercover work. I know what we have is much stronger than that, but I'll never be sure unless we give it some time and distance."

"That's bull," he grumbled. "How we met isn't what counts. It's how we feel now."

"I know, but I'm going to be trapped in a safe house

with round-the-clock guards for the next few weeks. I don't want you to be forced to live that way."

"You think I'll resent having to spend time with you? That makes me pretty shallow, doesn't it? Sounds like you just want to be rid of me while you reevaluate our relationship."

"I didn't mean it that way," she said on a sigh. "It's just not practical for you to go into hiding when you could be taking care of things at home. The agency will give you protection if you want, but Donald doesn't want me that far from D.C."

"You've talked to him and he's suggesting we don't see each other again until after Haroldson's trial?"

"He thinks it's the safest thing to do at this point."

Her lips found the pulse at his throat. When she sucked at his flesh, he drew in a breath and his body started to sing with anticipation. A rush of possessiveness nearly brought him to his knees. No other woman had ever given him so much or claimed so much of his soul. Her virginal innocence combined with her innate sensuality made him feel humble and needy.

"Maybe we can manage to rendezvous every once in a while, providing you're interested," she whispered.

Interested? He'd have to be dead not to be interested, but he had a feeling it wasn't going to happen.

Swinging her into his arms, he carried her to the bed, and then fell on it with her. He locked his arms around her and moaned with delight as she held on just as tightly. Everything else could wait until he'd found a physical release for all the pent-up emotion.

Then they could talk logistics.

Chapter 13

Paris, France

Steven studied his image in the mirror. Short, thin, balding and nondescript. That was the real Steven Partoll's reflection, but he never left France without a disguise. In all the years he'd traveled the world, he'd always presented a different, unmemorable facade. Interpol had a photo of him on file, as did the United States Federal Bureau of Investigation, but those images were just two of the many faces he'd used and discarded.

They called him Le Ferret, but he despised the appellation. It sounded more like a rodent than the powerful beast of prey he epitomized. He'd privately called himself Le Parisian, a proud, suitable nickname for a national treasure, he thought, his laughter echoing through the spartan apartment.

This would be his last job, and he'd decided to be himself. The idea was so ingenious that he laughed out loud. Who would ever suspect a mild-mannered, small-time tabloid editor of being a hired murderer? Who'd ever guess he topped Interpol's list of most wanted international hit men?

He planned to retire on the five million Haroldson had promised. The first million had already been deposited in his Swiss account. The rest would be transferred once the hit had been confirmed.

He'd considered taking the million and disappearing. Haroldson was in no position to come after him, he thought smugly, but even professional criminals had reputations to uphold. He planned to retire in a blaze of glory that no one would ever duplicate.

Besides, this would be the ultimate test, a challenge unlike any other. The hit would go down in a U.S. federal courthouse, with metal detectors, armed guards and FBI's finest agents. The job would be his swan song, his pièce de résistance. Others might view it as a suicide mission, but they didn't have his skill and daring.

He was the best, and this job would prove it. He intended to live a long and pampered life with the earnings from this final paycheck. He already had his sights set on a lush plantation in South America. He planned a complete physical transformation with the best plastic surgery money could buy. He'd grow a little opium for pleasure, buy the favors of some beautiful mademoiselles, and thumb his nose at international extradition treaties.

The woman.

He should have killed her years ago outside her family's burning home. He'd recognized her among the horrified bystanders, but it had been too late. He hadn't dared to draw attention to himself at that point, so he'd let her live.

It had been his first job, and he'd done it for a mere pittance. His brow creased at the memory. Haroldson had put a price on each family member's head, so he'd lied and sworn they were all dead.

She'd been a dent in his pride for years, but he'd been given a chance to restore his self-image. This job would prove, once and for all, that no man could match him in courage and cunning.

Viva le Parisian.

Chapter 14

Margaret Wilding owned an elegant old Victorian home along the craggy shoreline of northern Maine. At seventy years old, she was as weathered as the rocks along the waterfront, but still as strong and sure as the tides. She welcomed Rianna and Special Agent Payne with open arms and a minimum of questions.

After Rianna introduced her bodyguard and briefly outlined the situation, the older woman made them comfortable in her home and treated them like long-lost relatives.

For the next few weeks, the bodyguards came and went in a regular rotation, while the women developed even deeper bonds. Margaret's old house was in serious need of repair that she couldn't afford on her social security income. Rianna sold the jewelry she'd mailed from Somerset to fund a renovation. Then she threw herself into the project, desperate to fill the long hours of waiting and isolation.

When she wasn't working on the house, she spent a lot of time watching the water beat against the rocks and wondering about the purpose of life. She risked an occasional call to Kyle, but their conversations were brief and strained.

Tabone had never been apprehended, so her security was too tight to allow for a romantic rendezvous. She wondered if Kyle had some other less-complicated woman who was willing to warm his bed, but she couldn't find the courage to ask him.

While alone at Margaret's, she kept asking herself what she wanted from life. The answer remained the same.

Kyle Tremont.

She loved him, missed him unbearably, and badly wanted a chance for a normal relationship.

The blistering heat of the Texas sun had faded a bit as autumn progressed, but it still beat down on Kyle's head as he hammered another nail into the roofing shingle. His muscles strained and sweat glistened over his bare torso, but the hot, physically taxing work gave him a satisfaction that little else had these past few weeks.

It had taken a while to get all the insurance claims settled and even longer to get his house back to normal. He'd decided to rebuild it himself, and now the woodshop was nearing completion.

He'd thought the hours of backbreaking work would help keep his mind off Rianna, but he'd been wrong. Images of her filled his thoughts daily, sometimes hourly—her sweet, tantalizing smile, her sexy confidence and her iron determination to see justice served.

His isolated lifestyle no longer appealed. He ate because he needed strength, but he didn't enjoy much of anything. His sleep was restless, at best. His body yearned for its mate. The occasional phone calls just intensified his need for a more permanent arrangement.

The damage to his personal property hadn't been that devastating. Things just weren't important. He couldn't work up much enthusiasm for his business, though he'd tried to bully himself into caring.

He missed her more than he'd ever thought possible. He loved her, and it was his first experience with the deathless, aching kind of love he suffered. He'd cared deeply for Margie, but even those emotions seemed mild compared to the depth of feeling he had for Rianna.

He wasn't coping very well, and he wondered how she was dealing with the situation. Had she decided they had something worth fighting for or that he was just a means to an end? Now that her quest for justice would soon be complete, would she want independence more than commitment?

After weeks of slow, painstaking construction, he should be excited about the progress of his new workshop, but he couldn't think much beyond the progress of Haroldson's legal case. It was nearing time for the case to go to trial.

He still hadn't told her how much he loved her. Kyle asked himself why, as he lay in bed and ached for her. He'd been slow to recognize the emotion, slow to put a name to the feelings he experienced every time she smiled or spoke or made love to her.

He was in regular contact with the assistant U.S. attorney in charge of the case, availing himself for interviews and volunteering to back up Rianna's testimony. He'd submitted a detailed case report and undergone a lie-detector test.

She might not want him involved, but he was already in, heart-and-soul deep. He didn't trust Uncle Sam's best to protect her once she appeared in court. Her identity and location would be compromised by then, her every move monitored.

Kyle planned to do some monitoring of his own.

National and international news had been slow, so the media created a circus around the Haroldson case. Reporters for every major news operation had probed for details on the affluent banker and the undercover operative who'd posed as his fiancée. Rumors were rampant, though most remained unsubstantiated.

It was the stuff of TV movies and best-selling novels, so everyone and his brother wanted a piece of the action. Sullivan managed to get background checks on each reporter and photographer that was granted access to the courtroom. Security was especially tight, but Kyle had no trouble getting preferential clearance.

As the courtroom started filling for the first day of the trial, Kyle, Sullivan and a team of other agents watched each attendee as he or she passed through the door. They made sure every face was recorded on camera and mentally cataloged every man and woman who entered the room.

When the judge took his seat behind the bench, Kyle took his a row behind the railing that separated the galley from the prosecution table.

Rianna wasn't let into the room until everyone else had been seated. She'd reverted to her undercover disguise with platinum blond hair and blue eyes. She wore a demure blue suit with a plain white blouse, and looked like one classy lady.

Kyle feasted on the sight of her, absorbing every

nuance of her voice and re-exploring every beloved feature. She only allowed her gaze to meet his once, albeit briefly, but the awareness of each other's presence throbbed strongly between them. It was an emotional connection that he couldn't have described if his life depended on it.

His presence symbolized his support. He wanted her to be one hundred percent sure of him. He nearly burst with pride as she took the stand, and then answered hour after hour of questions in a calm, professional manner.

Her voice remained clear and firm as she related the personal tragedy she'd experienced and then the aspects of the case she'd been professionally assigned. For every accusation she made, the AUSA presented evidence to back it up. There were computer files, ledgers, videos and tape-recorded conversations between Haroldson and his staff. There were bank records, and evidence of money laundering in a six-state radius.

It didn't take a genius to realize she had the jury in the palm of her hand by the end of the morning session. A couple of jurors blinked tears from their eyes, while other expressions ranged from shock to outright horror. The looks they sent Haroldson were telling.

As much as he preferred to keep his attention on the government's primary witness, Kyle couldn't afford to watch her for very long. He listened intently, but kept his gaze roaming the room, searching each face and then searching his memory for any connection with Haroldson.

Despite Sullivan's efforts to minimize the risks, there were still too many strangers in the courtroom with too many cameras and too much high-tech equipment.

During the break for lunch, he and Sullivan compared notes. "Are you having the courtroom checked?" he asked Sullivan when the two of them met in the outer hallway.

"We're running metal detectors over every inch of it, every time we get the chance."

"Someone could use a plastic explosive."

"Which would kill Haroldson, too, and have a whole host of law enforcement agencies out for vengeance. Not to mention the media."

"You don't think Haroldson has associates who'd like to see him dead?" asked Kyle, his gaze perusing the throngs milling in the hallway.

"I'm sure there are plenty, but probably none stupid enough to pull off a hit in a federal courtroom. Still, we have dogs searching for anything out of the ordinary."

"Good," said Kyle. Then he changed the subject. "How's Rianna?"

"You mean our Mary?" asked Sullivan.

"I mean your star witness," came his terse reply. "I want to talk to her."

Sullivan raised his brows and stared at him for a minute. "I'll see what I can do, but only if she agrees."

"After court today?"

The deputy director hedged. "That might not be a good idea. Everybody who makes contact with her increases the danger. You know that."

Kyle would protect her with his life. He wouldn't let anyone hurt her, but he needed to see her and get close to her. Then he'd know if her feelings had changed.

"How long do you expect the trial to last?"

"At first, Haroldson's lawyers were in a big rush to go to trial in hopes of having the charges dropped or the case dismissed. Our case is too airtight for that.

Next, they'll try to discredit Rianna. Failing that, my guess is they'll try to lay the blame on one of Haroldson's other employees.''

Another agent poked his head out the door and gave them the all-clear to return to the courtroom. They had repeated their scrutiny of everybody that entered with each new session.

"By the way," Sullivan mumbled to him. "The code word is *dive*. If you see anything out of the ordinary, yell the word *dive* and Rianna knows to duck for cover."

"Will do."

"Tremont wants to see you," Donald told Rianna later that evening.

She'd moved from Maine to a safe house in D.C. for the duration of the trial, and he shared dinner with her.

Her breath faltered at the mention of Kyle's name. Seeing him in the courtroom had stirred a longing in her that wouldn't be appeased. Just one look at him had nearly been her undoing. She ached to talk to him, touch him and feel his arms around her. It had been weeks since they'd been together, but it felt like an eternity.

"I was a little surprised to see him there. He never told me he planned to attend."

She felt Donald's gaze on her face, but couldn't quite meet his eyes. Her emotions were too raw where Kyle was concerned, so she continued to pick at her food.

"He's not the sort of man you can easily dismiss. Nor is he one to wimp out of a difficult situation. He cares a great deal for you."

She hoped so. Dear heaven, she hoped he cared enough to wait for her and accept whatever lifestyle she might be forced to endure. His presence in the courtroom had given her spirits a much-needed lift. His silent offer of support had boosted her courage. She desperately wanted him in her future, but he'd never mentioned marriage. Maybe he wasn't sure enough of his feelings for her. The idea scared her almost as badly as did loving him.

"Did he say how long he was staying? Where? Or how he thought the trial went today?"

"He's staying as long as it takes, and I think he's bunking down at Special Agent Payne's apartment. The two of them have gotten chummy since they met at the cabin."

Rianna smiled faintly. The young agent had probably kept him apprised of the activity at Margaret's house. Payne wouldn't have given away any secrets, but he still could have shared information.

"I told him he could come here for a few minutes when Payne goes off duty."

Her heart raced at the suggestion, but she quickly controlled the excitement. As badly as she wanted to see him, she couldn't risk having her concentration shattered right now. She didn't dare give Gregory and his high-priced vultures an edge. His defense team would be after blood.

Their discussion was interrupted when the doorbell rang, followed by a knock. Donald told her to sit tight while he coordinated the changing of guard shifts. She heard the door opening and the hum of male conversation.

Restless and on edge, she cleared the table and filled the dishwasher. With her back turned to the kitchen door, she felt him before she saw him. The fine hairs on her neck tingled with awareness.

"Rianna."

Kyle's deep voice washed over her like the warmest of caresses. She closed her eyes and let the pleasure seep into her body. Nothing would please her more than to succumb to the comfort she knew she could find in his arms, but she forced herself to stay calm and controlled.

Turning, she gave him a smile, but she didn't cross the room to greet him or throw herself into his arms the way she wanted to do. A table and chairs, plus a whole lot of insecurity separated them.

"It's good to see you, Tremont."

His eyes narrowed and his jaw went taut. Rianna knew her lack of enthusiasm probably confused him, but she couldn't let her personal emotions distract her right now.

"Seems our relationship has seriously deteriorated if I'm back to being Tremont," he said.

"Do we still have a relationship?" she asked.

"I'm here, aren't I?"

"Yes, but we've been apart a long time." She nervously twisted a dishcloth in her hands. "I thought you might have someone else in your life now."

"There's no one else in my life or my bed, if that's what you really want to know. I'm not that superficial, and we have unfinished business between us."

Relief rushed through Rianna. She'd secretly feared he would tell her he wasn't interested anymore.

"We need privacy and some uninterrupted time to work things out. I just want to keep our relationship totally separate from all the ugliness of the trial. Does that make any sense?"

She watched some of the tension drain from Kyle. He nodded in acceptance. "We've waited a long time to put an end to Haroldson's reign of terror. It'll be over soon, and then we can discuss the future."

Neither his expression nor his tone gave her a hint at what he was feeling, but she was content to know he didn't plan to disappear once Haroldson had been convicted.

"Sullivan says we can get you out of the courtroom as soon as you're done testifying."

"No." She shook her head. "I don't want to miss any of it. I need to hear what the other witnesses have to say."

"You can always read the court transcripts. I'm not sure it's safe for you to be there unless you're testifying."

"What can possibly go wrong in a federal courthouse?" she asked. "I know you and Donald are doing everything humanly possible to keep it safe, and I can't think of anyone I'd rather have on my side. I'm not afraid." Her tone was more dismissive than she intended.

"Good." Kyle studied her for another long moment and then turned to go. "I'll see you in court."

It was hard to watch him leave, but Rianna knew it was for the best. At least, for now.

Kyle's skin crawled the next day as the judge pounded the gavel on his bench and started the proceedings. He had that prickly feeling he always got when something was dangerously wrong. Adrenaline surged through him as he scoured the courtroom for anything or anyone that seemed out of place.

He hadn't slept much last night. Seeing Rianna, yet

not being able to touch her had kept him too keyed up to rest. She hadn't given him much of a clue about her feelings, but at least she hadn't sent him packing. That meant there was hope. He just had to be patient until this damnable trial was over.

Most of the faces in the courtroom were the same as yesterday with a few variations of paparazzi. He knew Sullivan had checked and rechecked every person, but he couldn't shake the feeling that something sinister was present today.

Rianna took the stand again in the morning session for the cross-examination. Today, she wore a simple black dress that made her look cool and elegant. Coupled with the blond hair, she looked fragile, yet she continued to impress him and everyone else with her professionalism.

Haroldson's high-priced legal team was good, but they couldn't shake her unfaltering conviction that he was guilty on all charges. The only time her control wavered was when the lead defense attorney, Robert Fenton, started to badger her about her family.

"You were very young when your father worked for Mr. Haroldson, isn't that correct?"

"I was ten when my dad went to work for Haroldson, and he worked for him nearly two years."

Fenton, a distinguished, silver-haired man of sixty, continued in a pleasant, noncombative tone. "How would you describe your life during those two years? Pleasant? Your family prosperous?"

A small frown creased Rianna's brow. Kyle knew she was wondering where the questioning might lead. So was everyone else in the courtroom.

"I'm not sure what you mean," she replied. "I always thought we were a normal family. My father went to work on weekdays. My mother worked part-time at a grocery store. My brother and I went to school.''

''Would you say that your quality of life continually improved while your father was in Mr. Haroldson's employ?''

''Improved how?'' asked Rianna.

''Isn't it true that you moved into a nice new home, that your dad bought a new car, you got to buy a lot of pretty new clothes, and your family was generally more prosperous?''

''I think my dad was pleased with his salary, if that's what you mean.''

''What I mean is that your dad was spending more money than could be justified by his salary,'' said Fenton.

The AUSA protested. ''Objection, Your Honor. I don't see the relevance.''

The judge looked pointedly at Fenton.

''We intend to prove that Ms. Sullivan's testimony is tainted by her personal vendetta against my client.''

''That's a lie!'' insisted Rianna.

Fenton didn't hesitate, but turned his attention to the jurors. ''In order to defend my client, I have to prove that Ms. Sullivan's testimony is prejudiced. My client terminated her father's employment rather than file criminal charges against him, but she was too young to understand.''

''Objection, Your Honor!'' said the AUSA. ''Mr. Winthrop is not on trial here.''

''That's a twisted pack of lies.'' Rianna's heated accusation had the courtroom stirring with whispers and the judge pounding his gavel for quiet.

Kyle wanted to rip Fenton's throat out for deliberately baiting Rianna, jabbing at her tender recollections of her family, and attacking her where she was most vulnerable. He didn't like seeing her upset, and he wanted to strangle the arrogant defense lawyer. He willed her strength, and noticed that her spine stiffened and her chin hiked higher.

The ploy to rattle her backfired. When he glanced at the jury, he noticed that most of the jurors were glaring angrily at Fenton. Chalk one up for the good guys. If the legal eagles were smart, they'd get her off the stand instead of trying to discredit her.

Fenton and the AUSA spent a minute arguing with the judge, but then Fenton was allowed to continue.

He spoke directly to the jurors, his tone sympathetic. "Ms. Sullivan was only a youngster at the time. She can't be faulted for seeing Mr. Haroldson as the villain."

"The authorities brought charges against him," Rianna interjected in a tight voice.

Fenton turned back to her. "They were dropped as soon as another employee confessed."

"Which would have cleared my father, as well."

"We have no way of proving his innocence. This court, on the other hand, has the trusted word of an honorable man and a highly respected citizen."

Kyle glanced at Haroldson. His demeanor throughout the trial had remained cool and confident, but his eyes narrowed slightly when Rianna turned to stare at him. It was the first time she'd made eye contact with anyone other than the attorneys, so all eyes were on her. No man is his right mind could misunderstand the warning glint. She was getting more furious by the minute, so much so that Haroldson actually frowned.

"I wouldn't rely too heavily on your client's honor," she insisted, her voice holding a veiled threat.

"There was more than financial misconduct that sent my dad to the authorities."

"Don't believe a word she says!" shouted Haroldson. He shocked the courtroom by jumping to his feet and waving a threatening hand toward Rianna. "She'll do or say anything to protect her father's name."

The judge pounded his gavel again, quieting the stir of sensation caused by the unexpected outburst. Fenton moved swiftly to his client's side and urged him to sit down. They exchanged fierce whispers, and Fenton requested an extra few minutes to confer with his client.

Kyle had never seen Haroldson sweat, but he was sweating now. His expression was tight, his demeanor visibly agitated as he exchanged heated whispers with his attorney.

What did Rianna know that could shatter his smooth, practiced calm? It had to be something deeply personal, something that would permanently mar his public image, something that Haroldson feared even worse than the criminal charges against him.

While the defense team huddled around their client, Kyle took another slow look around the courtroom. The faces were mostly the same as yesterday, with a couple of exceptions. Sullivan had identified one of the new faces as Haroldson's sister. She sat on the defense side of the aisle. He knew she'd been subpoenaed to testify.

Another unfamiliar face was that of a tabloid editor from France. He was seated a couple of rows behind the defense table. As Kyle watched, the pale, thin man took a camera out of his case and began fiddling with the dials on it.

Something about the way the man handled the camera made Kyle tense. He watched as a small zoom lens began to protrude from the casing. The shape reminded him too much of a gun barrel.

At first, the editor had the lens pointed straight at Haroldson, but then he slowly angled it above his head and directed it toward the witness seat. All the fine hairs on Kyle's body stood on end.

Everything seemed to move in slow motion after that. Fenton declared his cross-examination finished, shocking everyone in the courtroom. The judge excused Rianna, but she was still bent on vengeance.

"What's the matter, Gregory?" she taunted. "Are you afraid I might mention the main reason my dad left your employ? That he caught you trying to molest his daughter?"

"You lying bitch!" Haroldson yelled, charging to his feet again.

Kyle watched in shock as Haroldson's head seemed to explode and his body crumpled.

"Dive!" he shouted, leaping to his feet and over the railing. He saw a second bullet shatter the wood of the witness seat, missing Rianna's head by inches as she dropped to the floor. Panic that he couldn't reach her in time had his heart pounding riotously.

All hell broke loose as he dove to cover her body with his own. He draped his arms over her head and buried his face in her hair, shielding her as much as possible as he dragged her under the prosecution table.

The courtroom erupted into pandemonium. Screams split the air along with loud shouts and a roar of mass confusion. Bodies were thudding against bodies in the rush to get out of the way. Kyle knew the guards at the door would be no match for the stampeding mob.

People fell to the floor all around them, some crouching under the same table. He stayed put, reassured by the feel of Rianna beneath him. Her heart pounded against his, the warmth of her permeating his clothes.

"Clear the room, but nobody leaves the building!" Sullivan's voice rose above the din. "I want all exits locked and guarded. Find a short bald guy with a dark gray suit."

Good, thought Kyle. They had an ID on the shooter. He'd made his getaway, but he'd never get out of the building. Sullivan's team had planned for every eventuality, and men were posted throughout the courthouse.

"Get the paramedics in here, and a forensic team." Sullivan continued to issue orders, and they could hear men scrambling to obey them.

Kyle listened, his heart racing, his body folded around Rianna's, until some sounds of normalcy returned. He didn't start to relax until the AUSA and his assistant rose from the floor. Once the room had been cleared, he finally moved his arms and spoke softly to Rianna.

"You okay?"

Her voice came in a puff of breathlessness. "You're squishing me."

Relief rolled over him like an avalanche, making his limbs tremble. Her gentle complaint was music to his ears. He propped his weight on his forearms, and slid lower until they were face to face, nose to nose. Then he just stared at her for a minute, savoring every feature.

"Sorry." He hadn't meant to crush her.

"No," Rianna said swiftly. She wiggled until she freed her hands, and brought them up to his face. "No, I'm the one who's sorry," she whispered, her heart in her eyes. "I'm so sorry I dragged you into this ugly mess."

Her touch sent heat coursing through him. Her words brought an ache to his chest. She shouldn't be apologizing for circumstances she had no way of controlling.

Right now there were more important personal things to deal with. He had so much emotion to express. There was so much to say, there were so many things crowding his mind. Things he should have said, but hadn't. Important things, life-altering things, all cluttering his thinking, quivering through his limbs and clogging his throat.

"I love you" was the only part of the turmoil he could verbalize.

He watched her beautiful eyes fill with tears, but the moisture didn't blur the love shining through. He felt it to the depth of his soul. Her response was little more than a whisper.

"I love you more."

"Impossible," he insisted huskily. "Kiss me." He needed the contact, the reassurance and the intimacy.

Their mouths met in a slow, sweet coupling that expressed hearts full of yearning. Kyle didn't want it to end. He wanted to keep her locked to him for all time, to feel her warmth and femininity, her generous heart beating against his own.

But they were rudely interrupted. "Hey, you two okay?"

They broke off the kiss and turned toward the voice. Sullivan had crouched beside the table. His grim expression softened a little when he saw them.

"We're fine." Rianna's reply was soft but sure.

Kyle cleared his throat. "I guess it's safe to surface?"

"Yeah, but it's not pretty."

The deputy director shifted out of sight again. Kyle reluctantly rolled off Rianna, then helped her crawl from beneath the table and stand. As soon as he saw what was left of Haroldson, he took her in his arms and pressed her face to his chest.

"What the hell happened?" he asked Sullivan.

"Apparently it was a hired hit man, and a damn good one. I don't know how the hell he got a gun in here, but I plan to get some answers if I have to personally beat 'em out of that lowlife."

"I saw the Frenchman pull out a camera. The gun must have been modified to fit in the casing."

"Well, it didn't impair the accuracy. If Haroldson hadn't lunged to his feet, the first bullet would have taken out Mary. Your warning and her quick reflexes saved her from the second one."

Rianna made a soft sound, and Kyle tightened his arms around her, folding her closer.

"Did you get the shooter?"

"Yeah, I just got word that he's in custody. He ditched the camera, but we'll find it."

"You need help?"

"We'll be fine. Why don't you two head to my apartment? I'll be there as soon as I have some answers."

Chapter 15

As soon as Kyle and Rianna closed the apartment door behind them, he ordered her to stay put and began a thorough check of the premises.

By the time he returned to the dimly lit foyer, she'd kicked off her shoes and tossed aside the blond wig. Her own hair felt limp. She fluffed it with her fingers, and then reached for the buttons of her dress.

Kyle approached slowly, his gaze raking her from head to toe, his expression going so dark and hungry that it made her heart pound. She loved him so much that she ached with it.

"Oh, no you don't, beautiful," he scolded, grabbing her hands to halt her stripping. He brought her fingers to his mouth and kissed them gently. "We're not rushing. As bad as I need you, we're not making love here. I want you naked in bed, where I can feel every inch of you against every inch of me."

Rianna had her own ideas about which of them

should be in control. The look in his eyes made her shiver with excitement. The touch of his lips spread warmth throughout her body. She wanted him, here and now.

Wrapping her arms around his neck, she drew him close. Then she looped a nylon-clad leg around his thigh and pulled him even closer. Their bodies pressed together in one slow, fluid move, every male angle burrowing into every feminine curve. Her blood heated at the feel of his hard, hot body.

Kyle slapped his hands against the door on either side of her head and leaned down to steal a kiss. But one was never enough between them. Each long, searching kiss slipped into another, and another, until they were moaning and writhing against each other.

"Bed," he insisted, dragging his mouth from hers. He crushed her against the door while his hands cupped her face. His eyes were turbulent with emotion—love, desire, and a need so fierce that it wiped all thought of resistance from Rianna's mind.

"My room's the one on the other side of the kitchen," she whispered, nibbling on the strong line of his jaw.

He swept her into his arms. "I know," he admitted gruffly. "I smelled you there."

Rianna trembled and held him tighter. She could never get enough of him. She loved his sensitivity, the sound of his voice, the strength and feel of his body, even his macho protectiveness. She loved the intensity of his desire for her. In that, they were well matched. She needed him just as desperately.

Kyle laid her on the bed and followed her down, pressing his body against hers while he cradled her head in his palms. His kiss was slow and deep and sweet. Rianna understood his need for reassurance. As badly as they wanted to make love, they didn't want to be parted long enough to rid themselves of clothes. They'd already spent too much time in forced separation.

When he finally ended the kiss, he leaned back far enough for their gazes to meet. The naked vulnerability in his eyes made her muscles turn to mush.

"Say the words again," he coaxed gruffly.

She knew what he wanted to hear. "I love you," she whispered, her throat going tight as she saw the way her admission affected him. He closed his eyes, but not before she saw the depth of his response.

"I love you," she repeated, feathering kisses over his face. "Now and forever. More than I ever thought it was possible to love anyone. More than I thought I had the courage to give."

"I love you that way, too," he declared in a voice rough with emotion. "I want you to be my wife. I want a lifetime to explore this love. What do you think?"

"Marriage—" Rianna faltered over the word. As much as she loved him, she hadn't dared to dream about marriage. He'd never so much as hinted at that type of permanency.

"When? Where? How? What about the case? Even though Gregory is dead, Donald will still need me to testify against the others."

"We can be married whenever and wherever you want. I'd rather it be soon, but we can work around the trials. Your life shouldn't be in jeopardy, so you don't have to be a slave to the system. Marry me," he reiterated.

Rianna badly wanted to believe. "You're sure? I

don't know anything about sustaining long-term relationships. What if I'm a terrible failure at it?''

Kyle's slow smile helped to ease her small spurt of panic. The confidence in his expression boosted hers.

"I don't have any experience, either," he confessed, sliding his hands down her throat to the open neck of her dress. He caressed the tender flesh, but his gaze stayed riveted to hers. "My folks were far from role models when it came to marriage, and I never put much effort into other relationships. But if you love me half as much as I love you, we can make it work. Nothing is impossible if we're together."

Rianna went limp under his caressing hands. "We're a helluva team, aren't we?" she whispered, her eyes filling with tears of joy.

"Perfect partners," he murmured as he slid down her body and began to re-acquaint himself with much-adored territory. "How about it? Willing to trust me with your future?"

"With my life," she returned softly. "My life, my heart, my soul."

"Your body?" Kyle teased, nuzzling her breasts.

Rianna laughed, tugged at his hair, and then set about convincing him just how much she trusted him.

Six hours and a lot of loving later, they were cuddled on the Sullivans' living room sofa. Donald had just stunned them with the news that the state had accepted Rudy's plea bargain. Tabone had been arrested and was expected to plea, as well.

The hit man refused to say anything, but the evidence against him was damning.

"You took a huge risk with that accusation you hurled at Haroldson," chided Donald.

"I know, but he made me furious. I would have kept his dirty little secret if he hadn't tried to save himself by tarnishing my dad's name."

"Apparently, Haroldson didn't care that the world might think him a murderer and a thief, but he couldn't bear the thought of being considered a sexual pervert," said Kyle.

"In his twisted mind, murder and fraud were all a part of a successful man's rise to power," said Donald. "Anything was acceptable when it came to prestige, but he knew that a child molester is considered the lowest form of life, even in prison. Whatever his psychological hang-ups, I'm glad the man's gone. All his army of thugs will run like rats."

"It's finally over," whispered Rianna. A chill raced down her spine, but the warmth of Kyle's embrace swiftly comforted her.

"For the most part," Donald agreed. "You may still be called to testify, but your safety shouldn't be an issue."

"It's time to put it behind me and get on with my life."

"Amen," said Donald. "Have any idea what that means in terms of your job?"

"She'll be moving to Texas," said Kyle.

Donald frowned. "What do you mean, moving?"

Rianna laughed softly. "He's not suggesting anything immoral," she teased. "He's asked me to be his wife, and I've agreed. I'll need someone to give me away and some help organizing a small wedding."

"A small wedding that can be organized in a couple of weeks," added Kyle.

"Sophie'll have heart failure," said Donald, grinning widely. "She'll want the whole shebang with

bridesmaids and tuxedos and towering wedding cakes.
I think she's already made some plans.''

Rianna and Kyle both shook their heads, then looked
into each other's eyes for a minute that stretched into
two and then longer.

Donald finally cleared his throat to regain their attention. ''I'll let you work out the details. If you want
to get married right away, we can pull it off somehow.''

''Do you think you could check about getting me a
position in the El Paso field office?''

''I think that can probably be arranged, but it might
take some time.''

''Good,'' said Kyle. ''We're thinking about a very
long honeymoon.''

Donald chuckled and bade them a good night.

Rianna turned into Kyle's arms and snuggled closer.
She loved the warm, solid feel of him. She couldn't
get enough of him. He seemed to feel the same way,
and she couldn't remember ever being happier.

It had taken her more than a decade, but she'd finally
accomplished two very important objectives in life.
She'd revealed Gregory Haroldson for the murderous
criminal she knew him to be, finishing the job her dad
had started. And as a bonus, she'd found Kyle, her
protector, lover and soul mate.

''What's on your mind?'' asked Kyle. ''You've gotten awful quiet.''

He used his nose to stroke the sensitive underside of
her chin, and Rianna arched her neck, granting him
better access.

''I was just thinking about how lucky I am,'' she
said. Then she murmured her approval of his caresses.
Goose bumps shivered down her back as he nibbled at

her throat. All he had to do was touch her, and she quivered with need.

"Luck had nothing to do with it," he argued. "Years of hard work and dedication are what got the job done."

Rianna smiled and slid her mouth over his jaw. "I wasn't talking about Gregory. He's out of my life forever. He's part of my past, and I refuse to allow him to clutter my thoughts anymore."

"Sounds good to me," he agreed, his tongue flicking out to bathe her lips. "I wouldn't care if I never heard his name again, either. He's history."

"Right," she mumbled, all thoughts of anyone but Kyle sliding from her mind.

She wanted more kisses. He tasted so good, and felt so hot. Her endless need for him would have been worrisome if it weren't being totally reciprocated. She no longer harbored any doubts about that fact. What Kyle couldn't put into words, he'd expressed with his touch. She'd never felt so loved.

He shifted until he lay flat on the sofa with her on top of him. His hands roamed slowly along her back and thighs. Their bodies were perfectly aligned, perfectly attuned.

"So why are you feeling lucky?" he asked.

"You," she murmured against his mouth. "Just you."

* * * * *

BOOK Offer Exclusive to Silhouette Romance Series

Buy this book and get another free! Simply indicate which series you are interested in by ticking the box and we'll send you a FREE book.
Please tick only one box

Special Edition	❏	Superromance	❏
Sensation	❏	Intrigue	❏
Desire	❏	Spotlight	❏

Please complete the following:

Name _____

Address _____

_____ Postcode _____

Please cut out and return the above coupon along with your till receipt to:

**Silhouette Free Book competition,
Reader Service
FREEPOST NAT 10298, Richmond,
Surrey TW9 1BR**

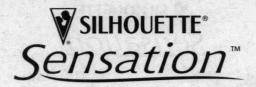

SILHOUETTE®
Sensation™

proudly presents an exhilarating new series

Shivers

Adventure, excitement and
supernatural love...

*Perfect for fans of Buffy, Anne Rice, Kelly
Armstrong and The Pirates of the Caribbean*

DARKNESS CALLS by Caridad Piñeiro
January 2005
A vampire helps an FBI agent find a psychotic killer,
and promises her eternal love.

ONE EYE OPEN by Karen Whiddon
April 2005
Can love blossom between a scarred man and
a female werewolf?

GHOST OF A CHANCE by Nina Bruhns
July 2005
A writer gets more than she bargains for when she
meets the man of her dreams—a sexy pirate ghost
under a 200 year old curse!

0105/SH/LC101

0205/SH/LC103

SILHOUETTE®
Sensation™

is proud to present
an exciting new series from popular author

LYN STONE

DANGEROUS. DEADLY. DESIRABLE.

Six top agents with unparalleled skills are
united to create an unbeatable team.

Their mission: eliminate terrorist threats
to the US – at home and abroad.

DOWN TO THE WIRE

February 2005

AGAINST THE WALL

April 2005

UNDER THE GUN

June 2005

Visit our website at www.silhouette.co.uk

FREE!

4 Books
and a surprise gift!

We would like to take this opportunity to thank you for reading this Silhouette® book by offering you the chance to take FOUR more specially selected titles from the Sensation™ series absolutely FREE! We're also making this offer to introduce you to the benefits of the Reader Service™—

- ★ **FREE home delivery**
- ★ **FREE gifts and competitions**
- ★ **FREE monthly Newsletter**
- ★ **Exclusive Reader Service offers**
- ★ **Books available before they're in the shops**

Accepting these FREE books and gift places you under no obligation to buy. you may cancel at any time. even after receiving your free shipment. Simply complete your details below and return the entire page to the address below. You don't even need a stamp!

YES! Please send me 4 free Sensation books and a surprise gift. I understand that unless you hear from me. I will receive 6 superb new titles every month for just £3.05 each. postage and packing free. I am under no obligation to purchase any books and may cancel my subscription at any time. The free books and gift will be mine to keep in any case.

S5ZEF

Ms/Mrs/Miss/Mr ....Initials..............................

BLOCK CAPITALS PLEASE

Surname...

Address...

....Postcode.............................

Send this whole page to:
UK: FREEPOST CN81, Croydon, CR9 3WZ